ALIEN NATE

DAVE WHAMOND

KIDS CAN PRESS

For my parents, who put up with my childhood obsessions with UFOs, conspiracy theories, aliens and Bigfoot. Wait, maybe Bigfoot is an alien! Oops ... I'm doing it again ...

Text and illustrations © 2020 Dave Whamond

Kids Can Press gratefully acknowledges the financial support of the Government of Ontario, through Ontario Creates; the Ontario Arts Council; the Canada Council for the Arts; and the Government of Canada for our publishing activity.

Published in Canada and the U.S. by Kids Can Press Ltd.
25 Dockside Drive, Toronto, ON M5A 0B5

Kids Can Press is a Corus Entertainment Inc. company

www.kidscanpress.com

The artwork in this book was rendered in pen and ink and digital watercolor.
The text is set in Boudoir and Blambot FXPro.

Edited by Jennifer Stokes
Designed by Michael Reis

Printed and bound in Shenzhen, China, in 10/2019 by C & C Offset

CM 20 0 9 8 7 6 5 4 3 2 1

Library and Archives Canada Cataloguing in Publication

Title: Alien Nate / written and illustrated by Dave Whamond.
Names: Whamond, Dave, author, illustrator.
Identifiers: Canadiana 20190094648 | ISBN 9781525302091 (hardcover)
Subjects: LCGFT: Graphic novels.
Classification: LCC PN6733.W43 A78 2020 | DDC j741.5/971 — dc23

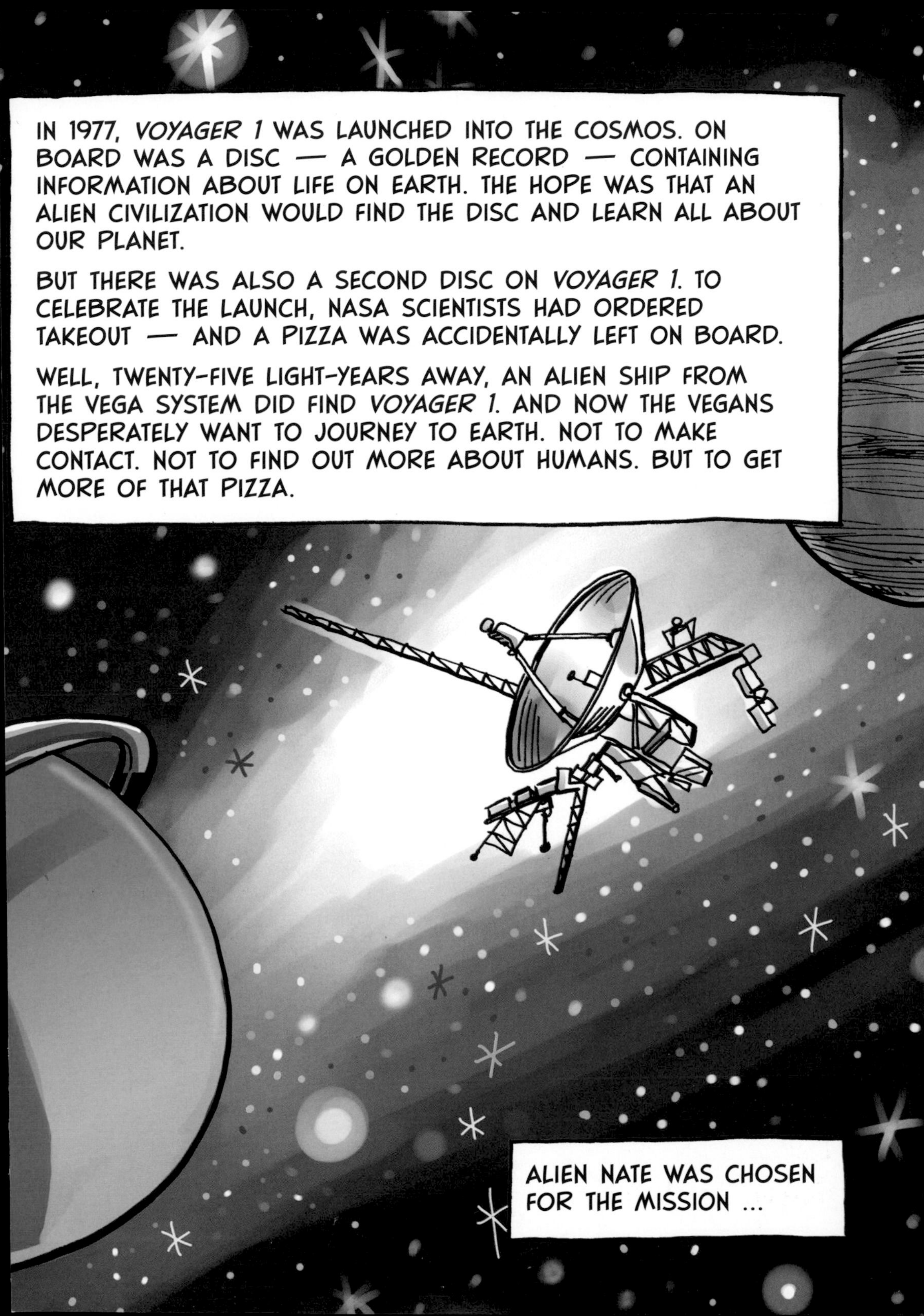
IN 1977, *VOYAGER 1* WAS LAUNCHED INTO THE COSMOS. ON BOARD WAS A DISC — A GOLDEN RECORD — CONTAINING INFORMATION ABOUT LIFE ON EARTH. THE HOPE WAS THAT AN ALIEN CIVILIZATION WOULD FIND THE DISC AND LEARN ALL ABOUT OUR PLANET.
BUT THERE WAS ALSO A SECOND DISC ON *VOYAGER 1*. TO CELEBRATE THE LAUNCH, NASA SCIENTISTS HAD ORDERED TAKEOUT — AND A PIZZA WAS ACCIDENTALLY LEFT ON BOARD.
WELL, TWENTY-FIVE LIGHT-YEARS AWAY, AN ALIEN SHIP FROM THE VEGA SYSTEM DID FIND *VOYAGER 1*. AND NOW THE VEGANS DESPERATELY WANT TO JOURNEY TO EARTH. NOT TO MAKE CONTACT. NOT TO FIND OUT MORE ABOUT HUMANS. BUT TO GET MORE OF THAT PIZZA.
ALIEN NATE WAS CHOSEN FOR THE MISSION ...

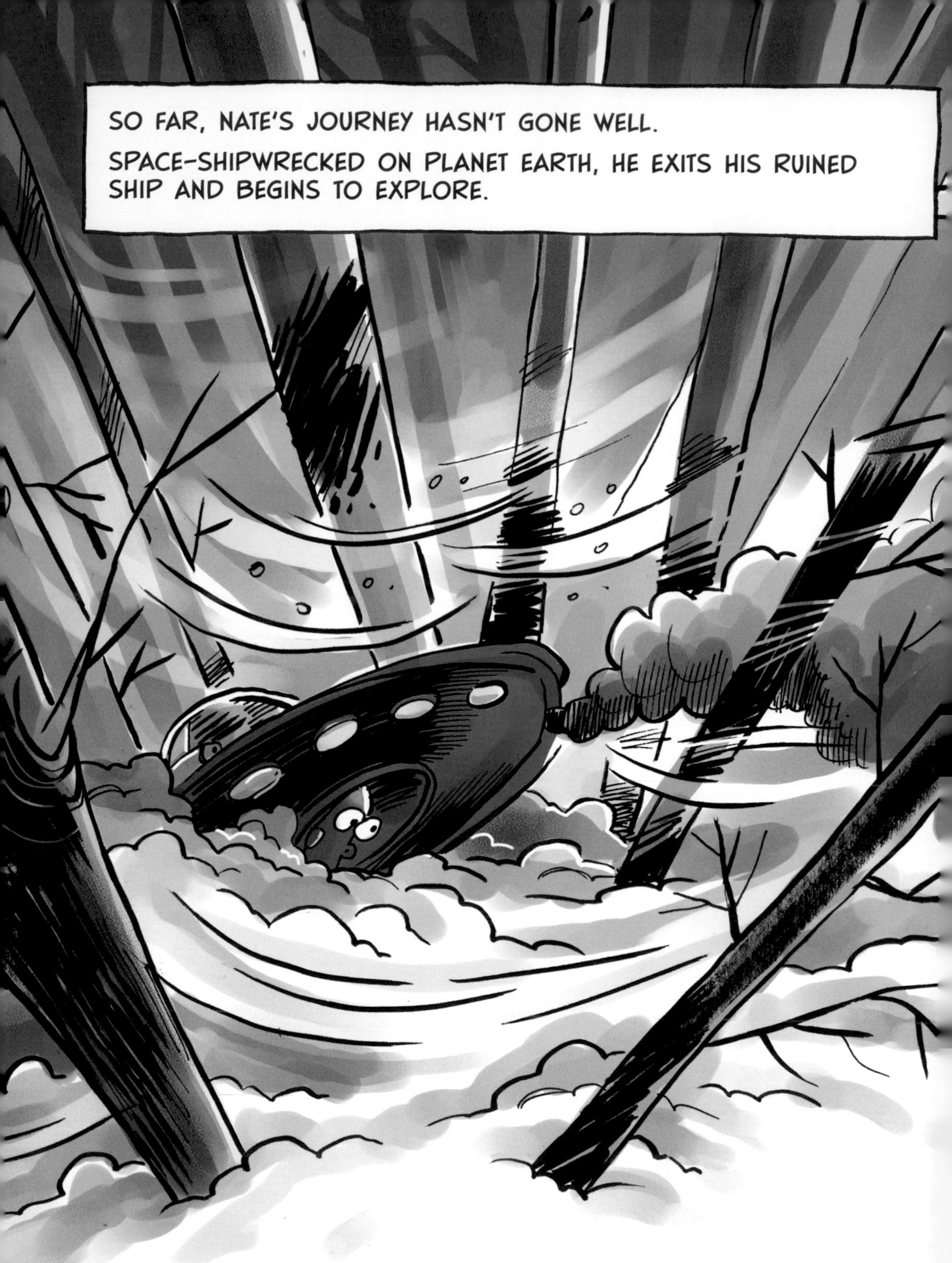
SO FAR, NATE'S JOURNEY HASN'T GONE WELL.
SPACE-SHIPWRECKED ON PLANET EARTH, HE EXITS HIS RUINED SHIP AND BEGINS TO EXPLORE.

AFTER PICKING UP A LOCAL RADIO BROADCAST, NATE RECORDS OBSERVATIONS IN HIS JOURNAL.

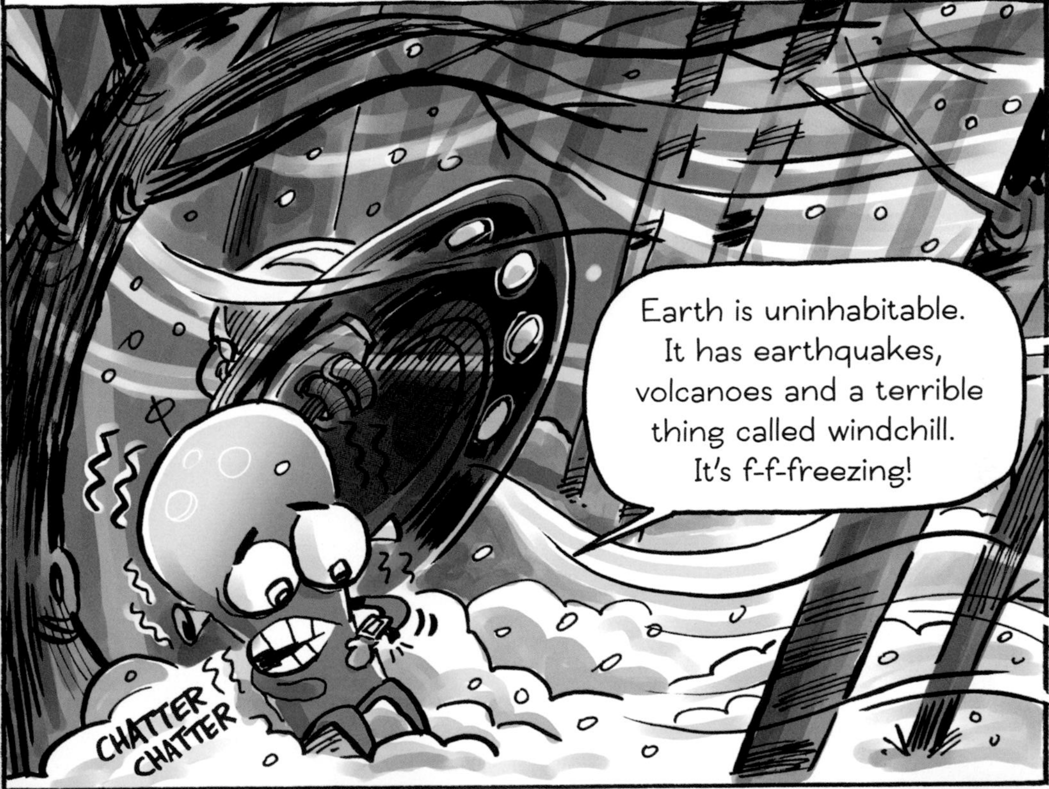
Earth is uninhabitable. It has earthquakes, volcanoes and a terrible thing called windchill. It's f-f-freezing!
CHATTER CHATTER

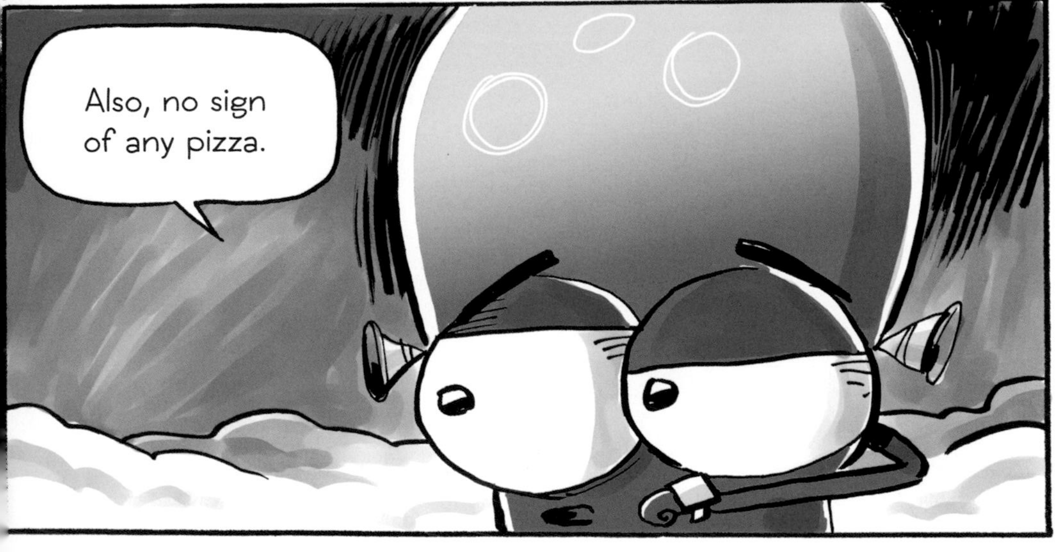
Also, no sign of any pizza.

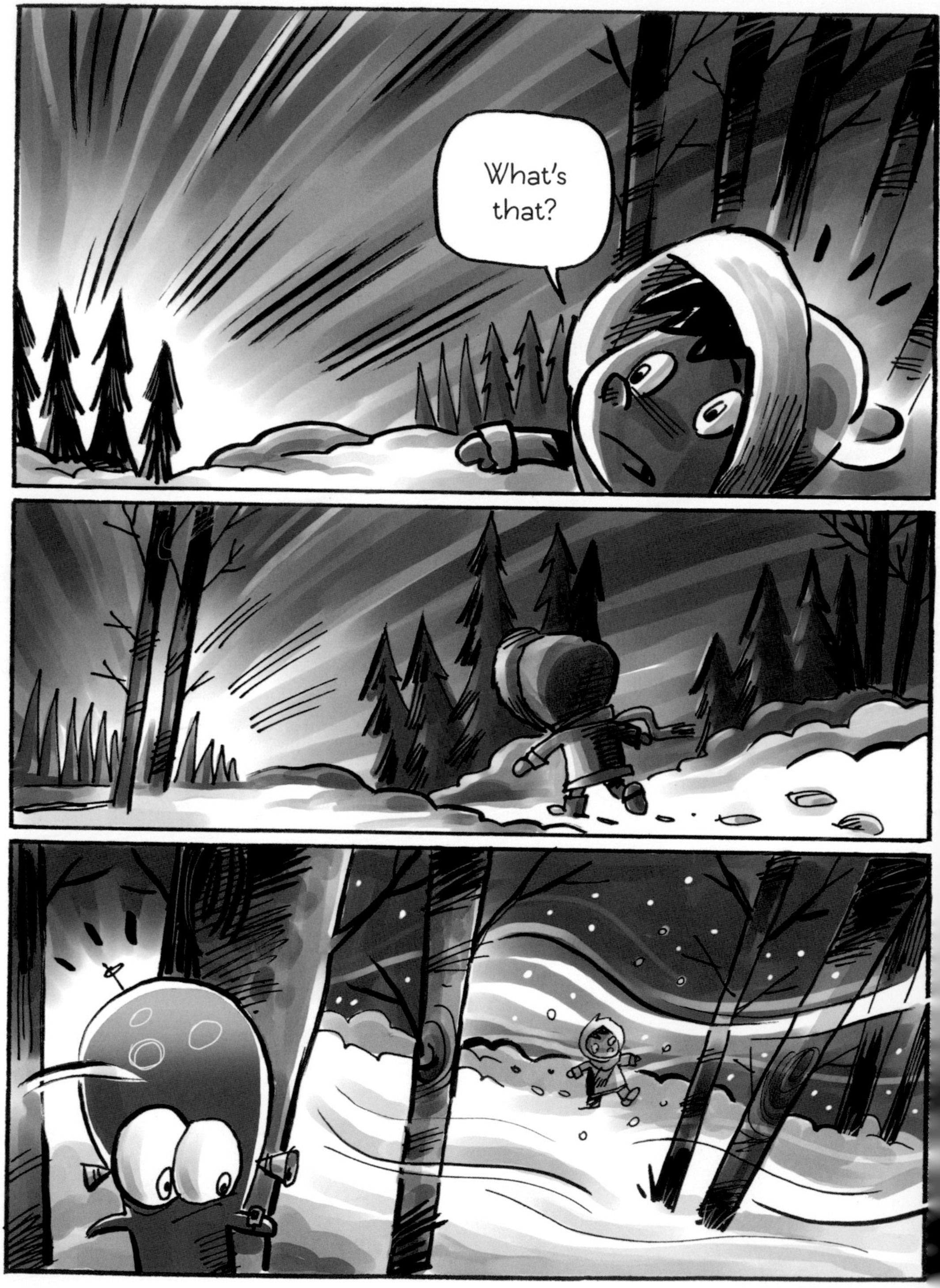
What's
that?

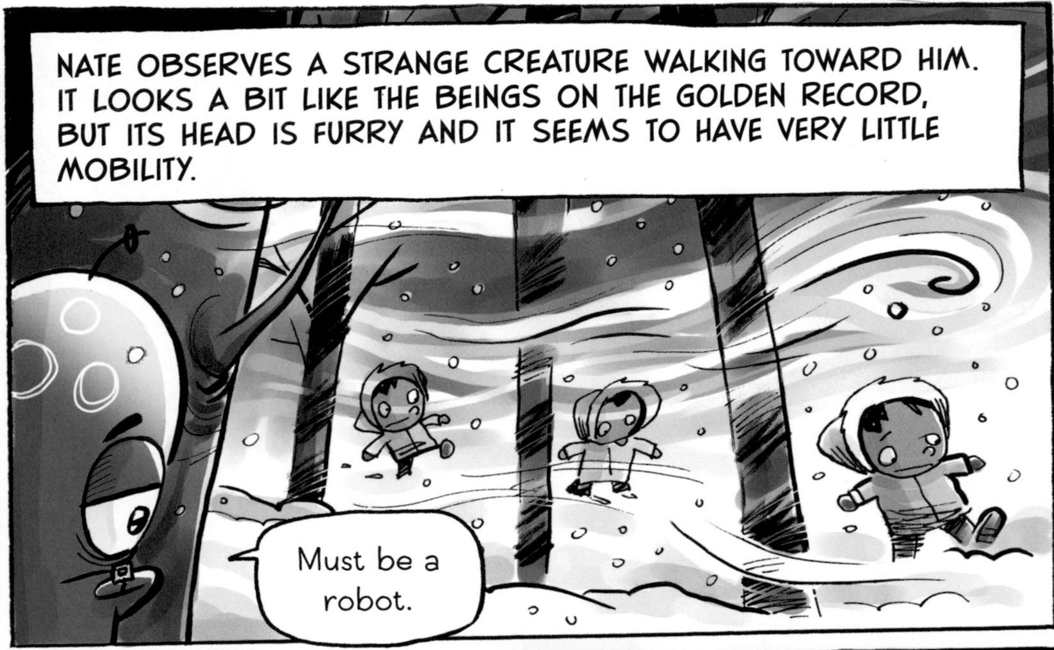
NATE OBSERVES A STRANGE CREATURE WALKING TOWARD HIM. IT LOOKS A BIT LIKE THE BEINGS ON THE GOLDEN RECORD, BUT ITS HEAD IS FURRY AND IT SEEMS TO HAVE VERY LITTLE MOBILITY.
Must be a robot.

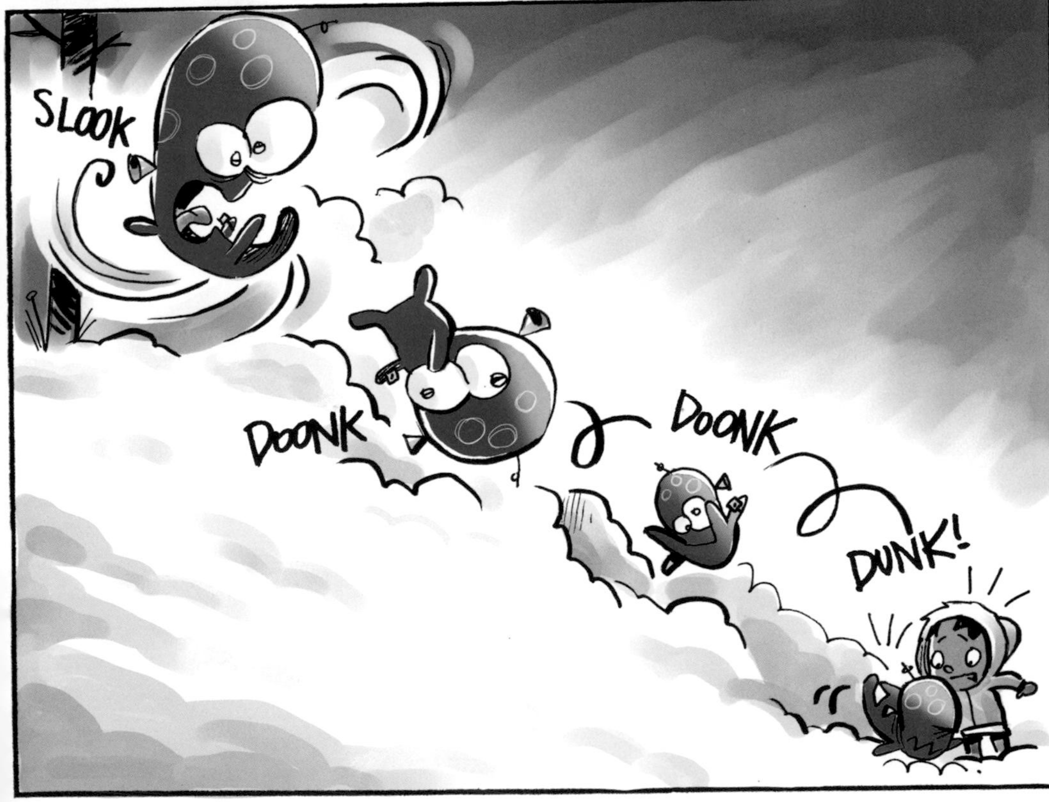
SLOOK
DOONK
DOONK
DUNK!

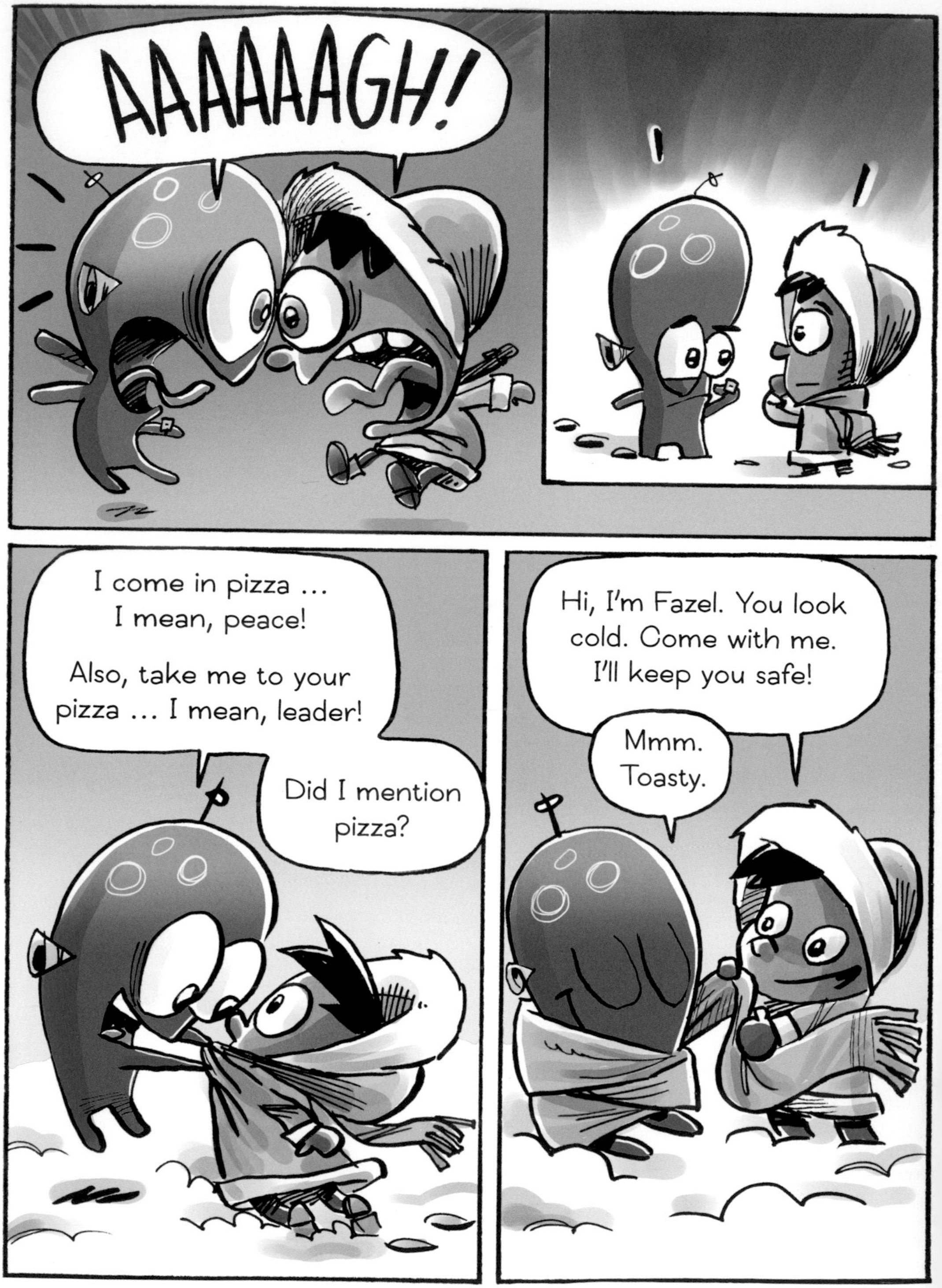
AAAAAAGH!
I come in pizza ... I mean, peace!
Also, take me to your pizza ... I mean, leader!
Did I mention pizza?
Hi, I'm Fazel. You look cold. Come with me. I'll keep you safe!
Mmm. Toasty.

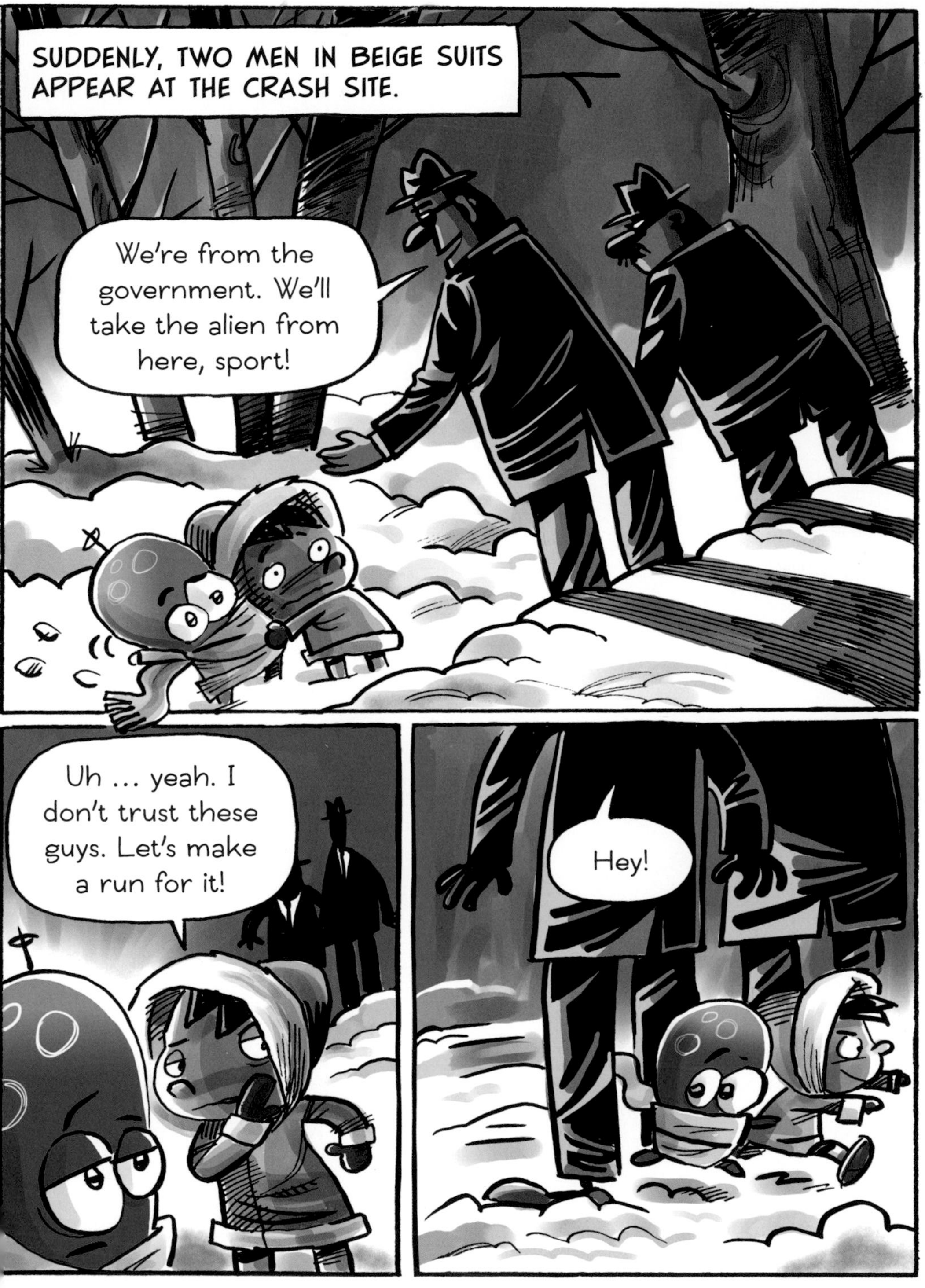
SUDDENLY, TWO MEN IN BEIGE SUITS APPEAR AT THE CRASH SITE.
We're from the government. We'll take the alien from here, sport!
Uh ... yeah. I don't trust these guys. Let's make a run for it!
Hey!

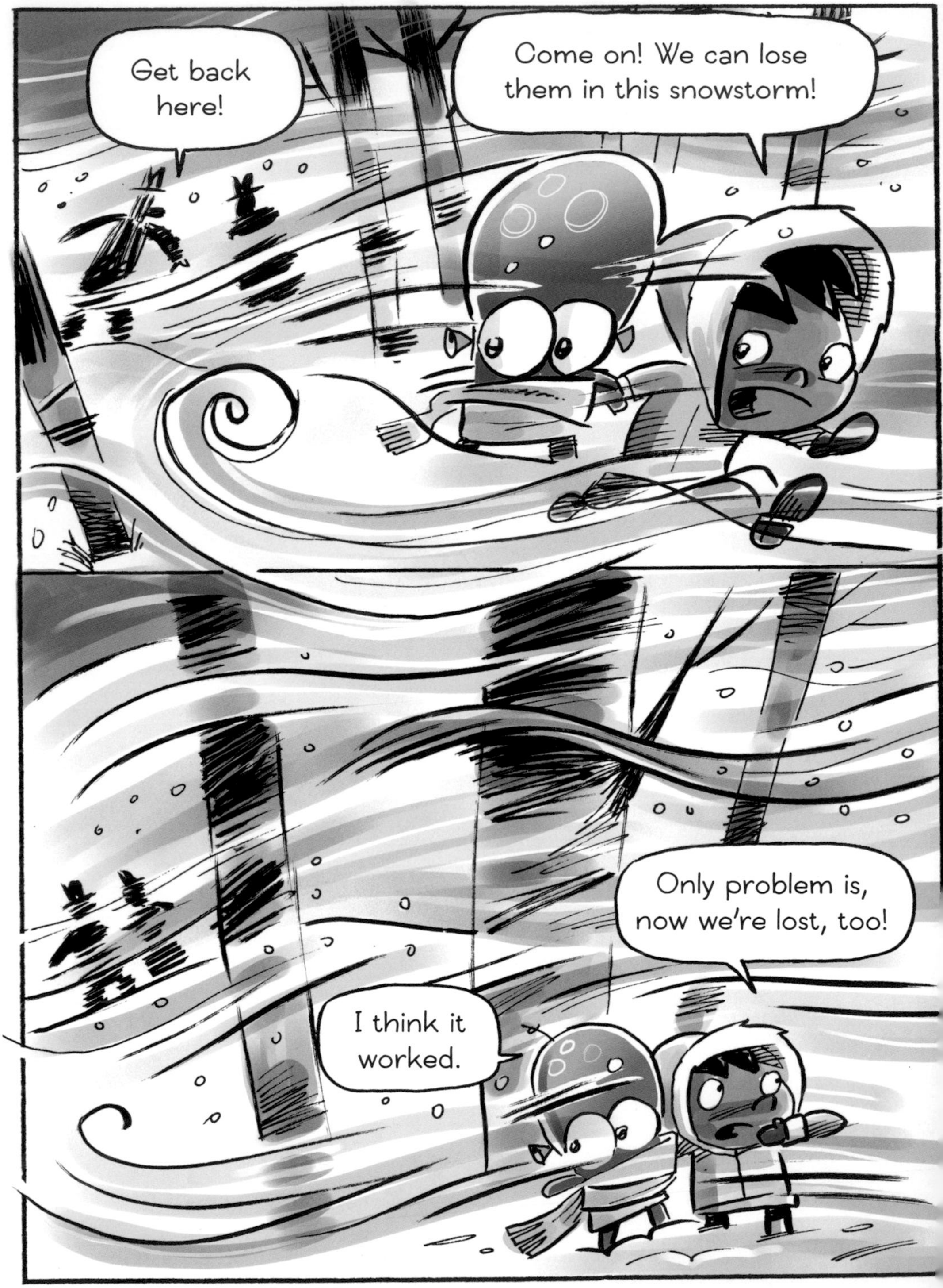
Get back here!
Come on! We can lose them in this snowstorm!
Only problem is, now we're lost, too!
I think it worked.

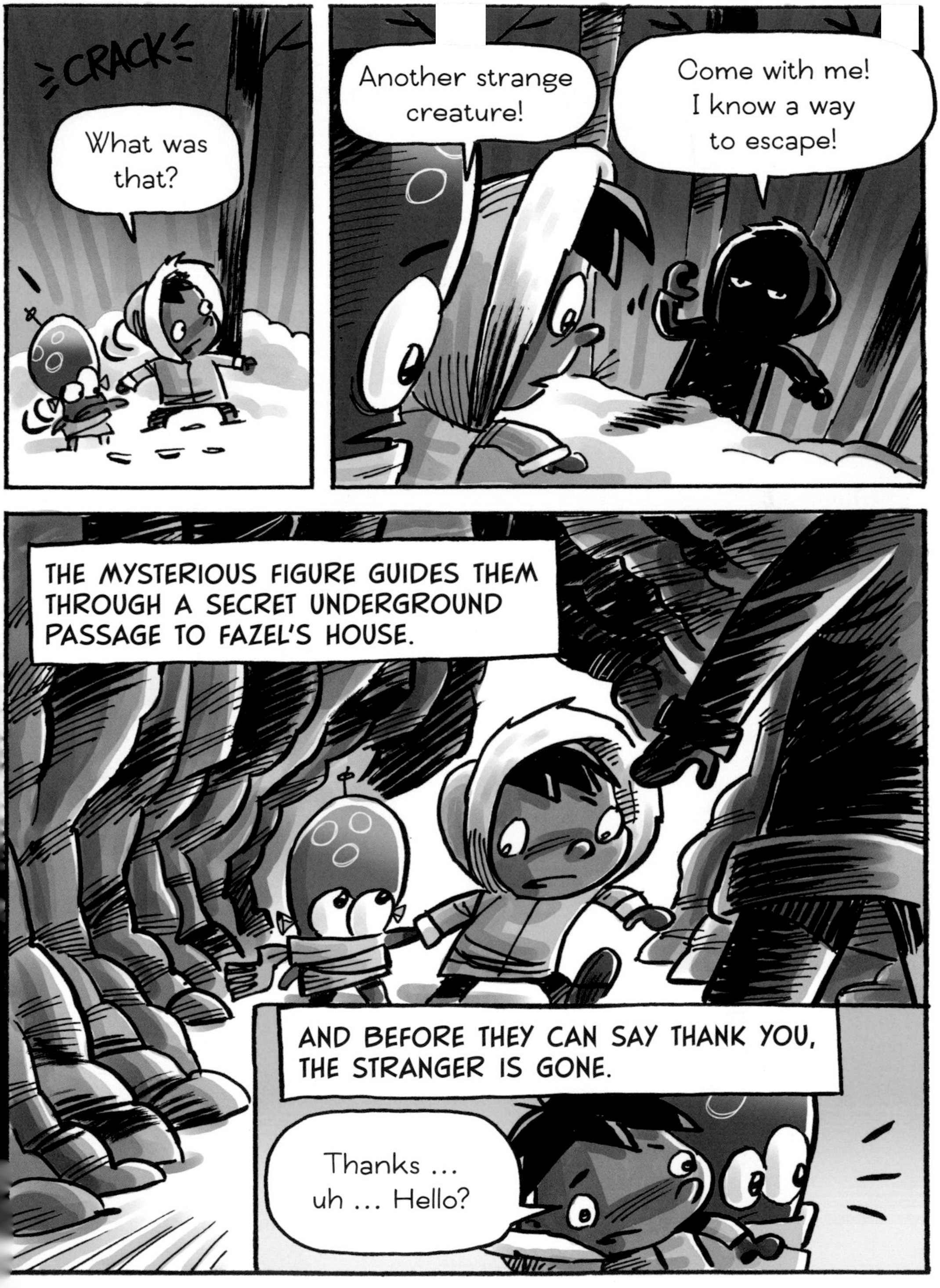

CRACK
What was that?
Another strange creature!
Come with me! I know a way to escape!
THE MYSTERIOUS FIGURE GUIDES THEM THROUGH A SECRET UNDERGROUND PASSAGE TO FAZEL'S HOUSE.
AND BEFORE THEY CAN SAY THANK YOU, THE STRANGER IS GONE.
Thanks … uh … Hello?

FAZEL OFFERS NATE A PLACE TO STAY UNTIL HE'S ABLE TO FIND A WAY TO FIX HIS SPACESHIP AND GET BACK HOME.

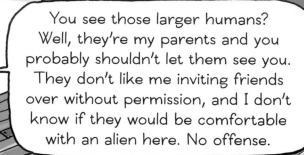

You see those larger humans? Well, they're my parents and you probably shouldn't let them see you. They don't like me inviting friends over without permission, and I don't know if they would be comfortable with an alien here. No offense.

Got it! Somehow, I don't think they've noticed me yet ...

SAFE AT FAZEL'S HOUSE, THE TWO BECOME FAST FRIENDS.

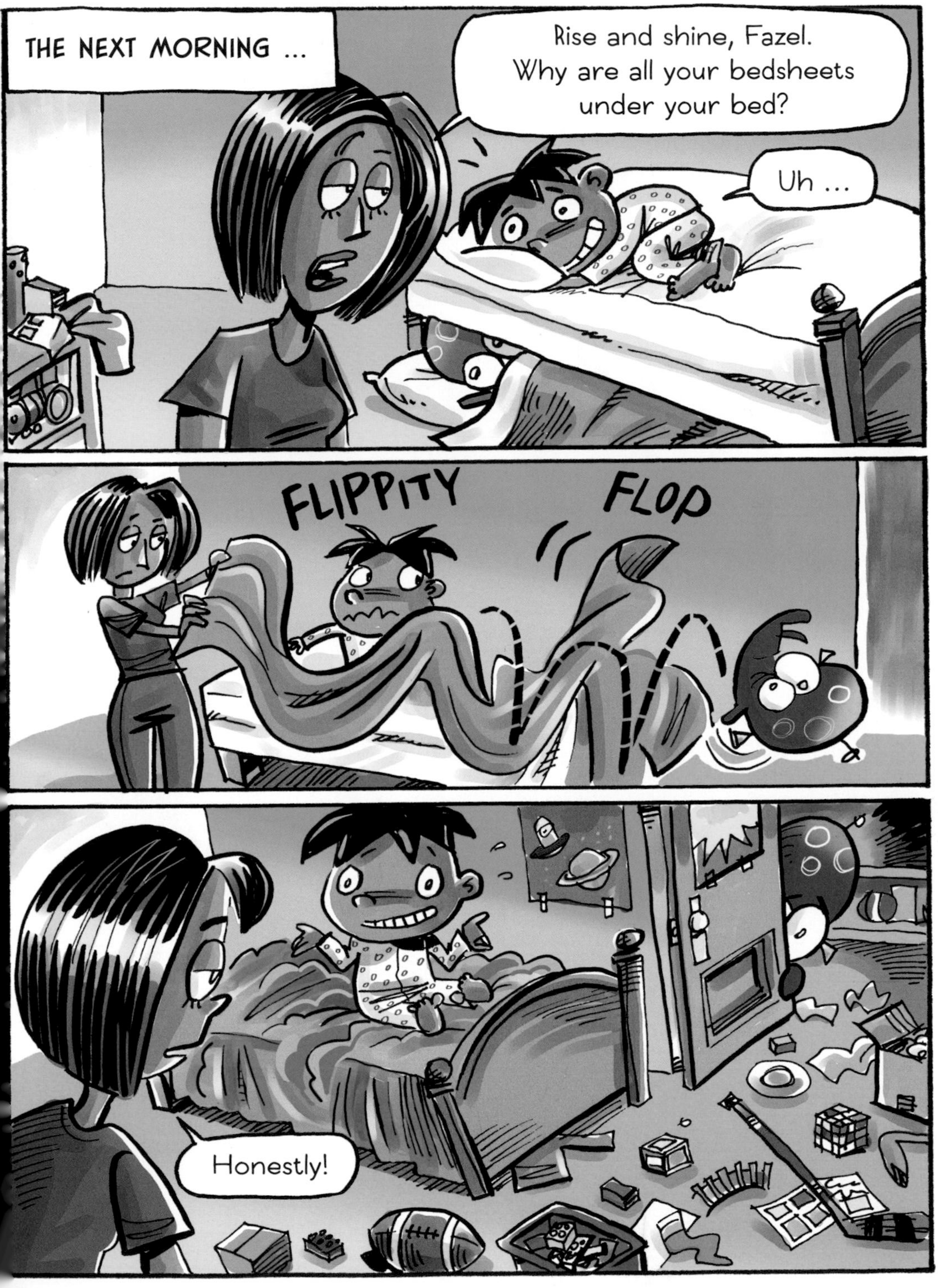
THE NEXT MORNING ...
Rise and shine, Fazel. Why are all your bedsheets under your bed?
Uh ...
FLIPPITY
FLOP
Honestly!

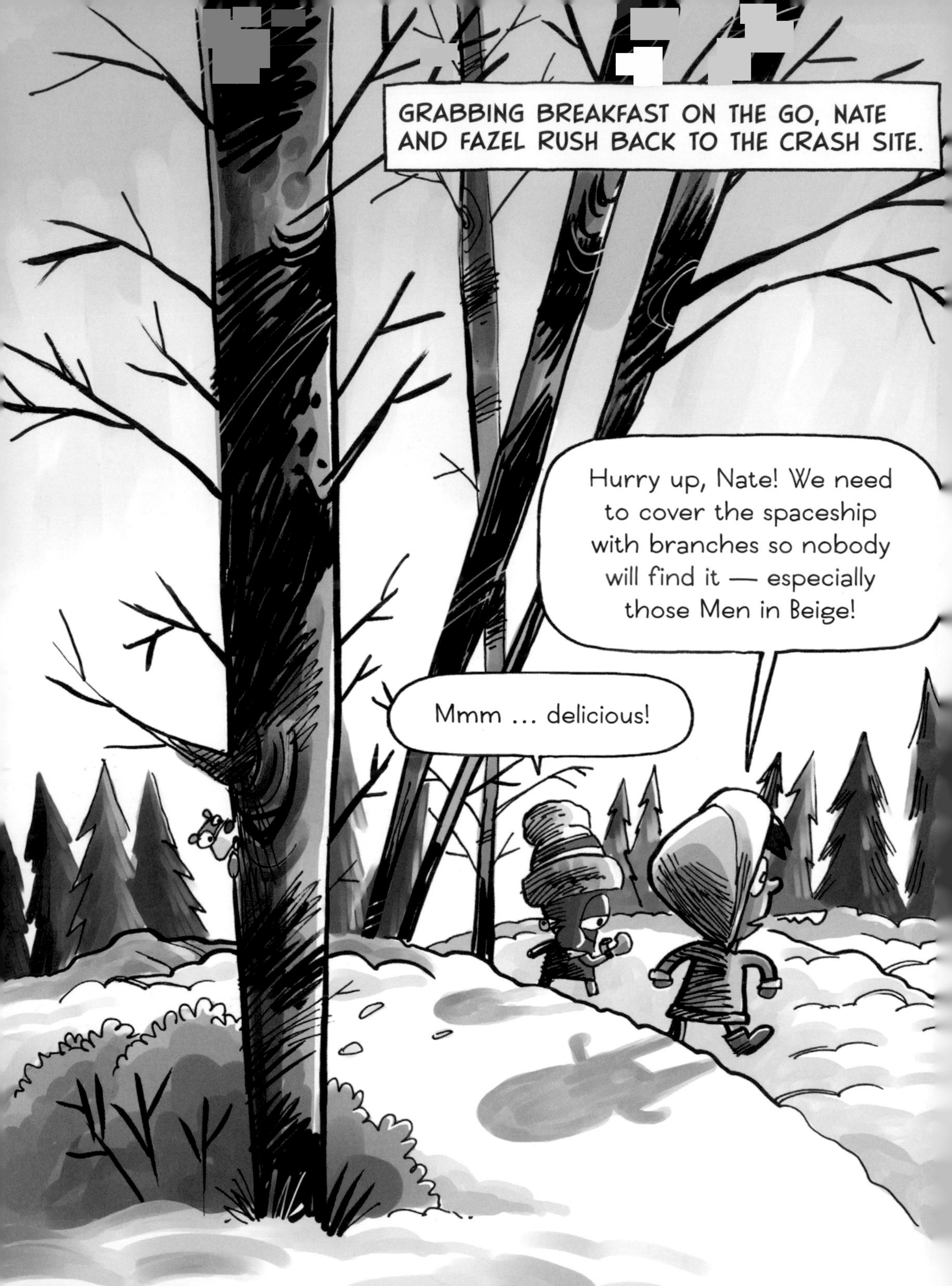
GRABBING BREAKFAST ON THE GO, NATE AND FAZEL RUSH BACK TO THE CRASH SITE.
Hurry up, Nate! We need to cover the spaceship with branches so nobody will find it — especially those Men in Beige!
Mmm ... delicious!

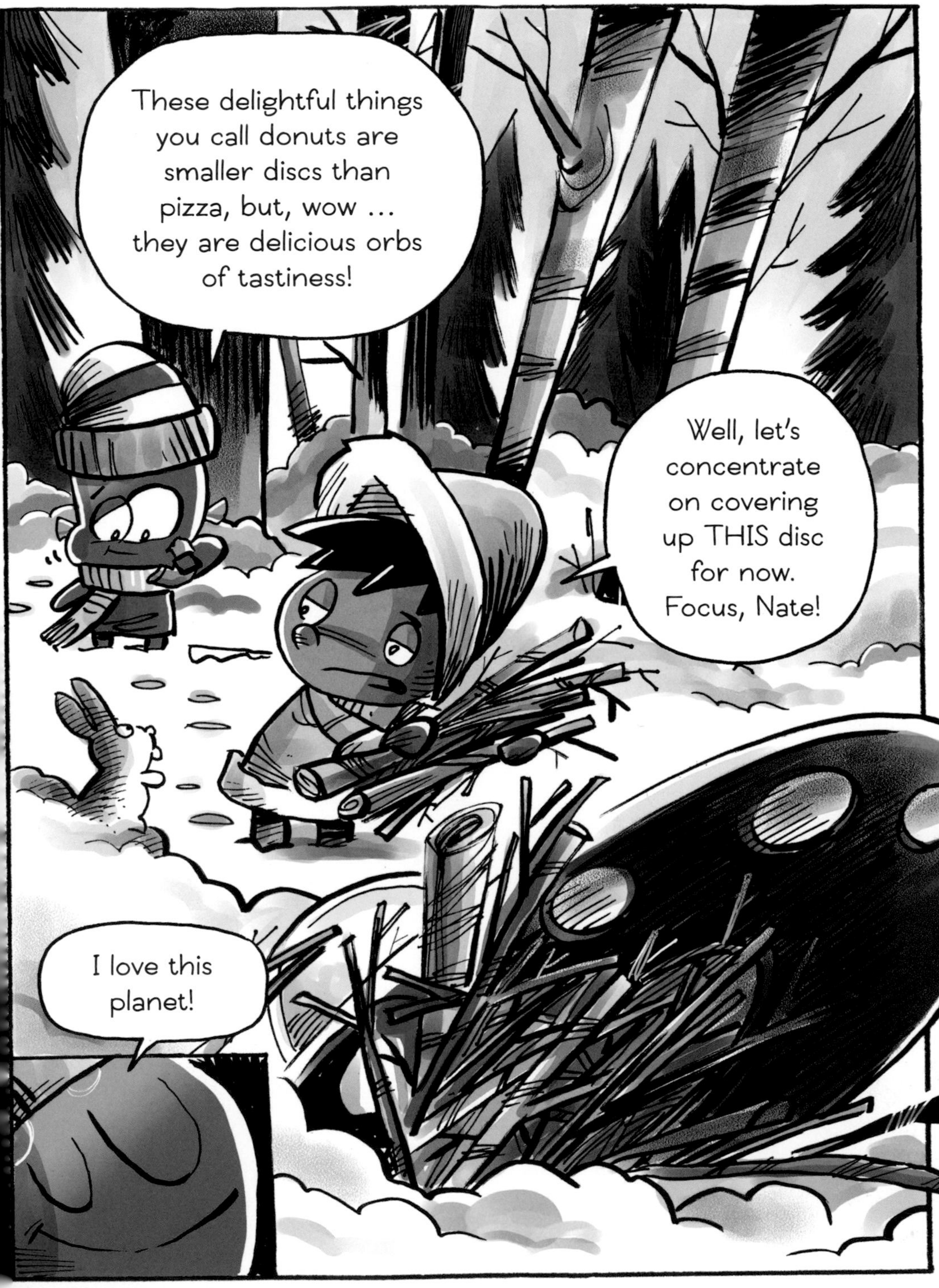
These delightful things you call donuts are smaller discs than pizza, but, wow ... they are delicious orbs of tastiness!
Well, let's concentrate on covering up THIS disc for now. Focus, Nate!
I love this planet!

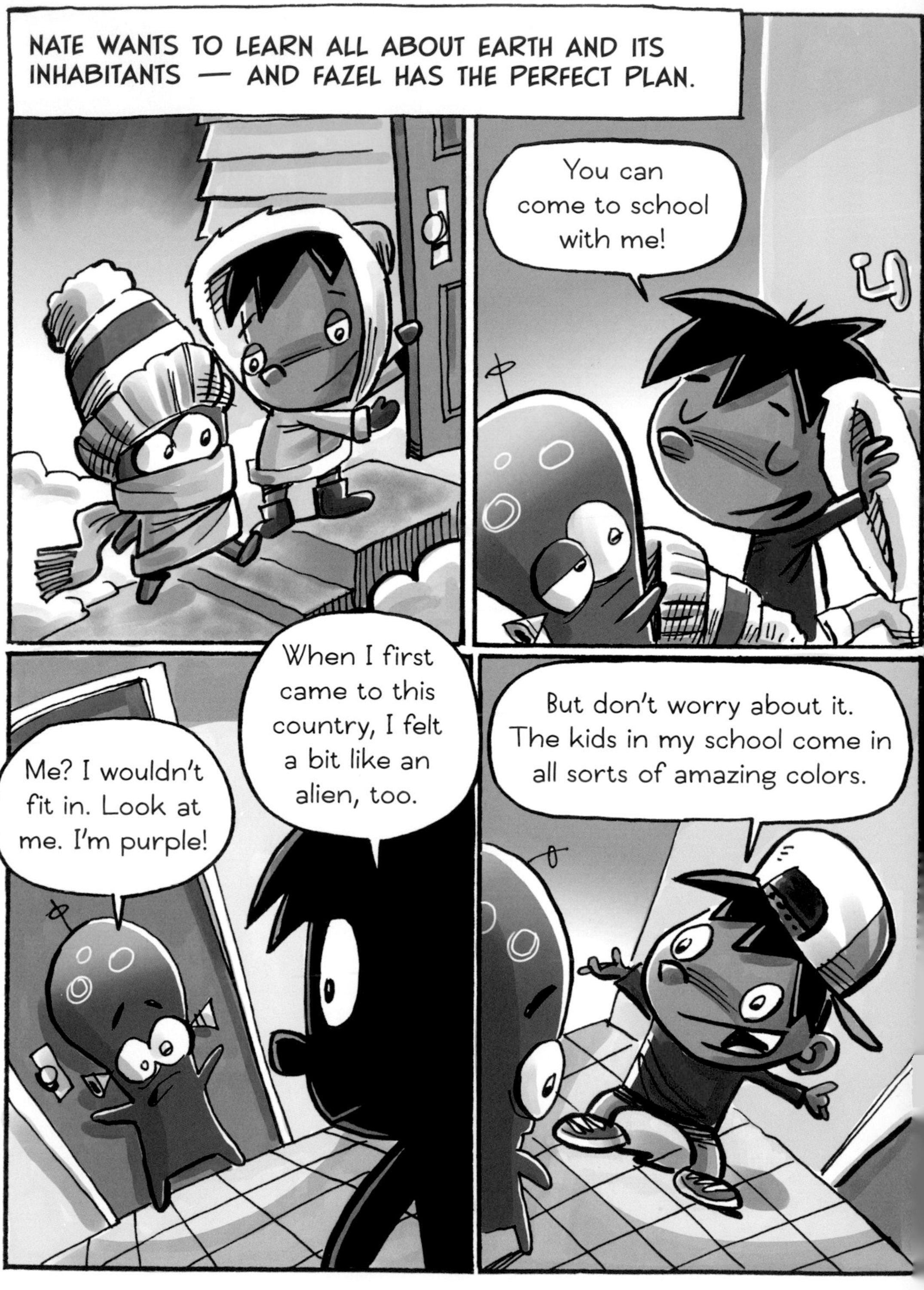
NATE WANTS TO LEARN ALL ABOUT EARTH AND ITS INHABITANTS — AND FAZEL HAS THE PERFECT PLAN.
You can come to school with me!
Me? I wouldn't fit in. Look at me. I'm purple!
When I first came to this country, I felt a bit like an alien, too.
But don't worry about it. The kids in my school come in all sorts of amazing colors.

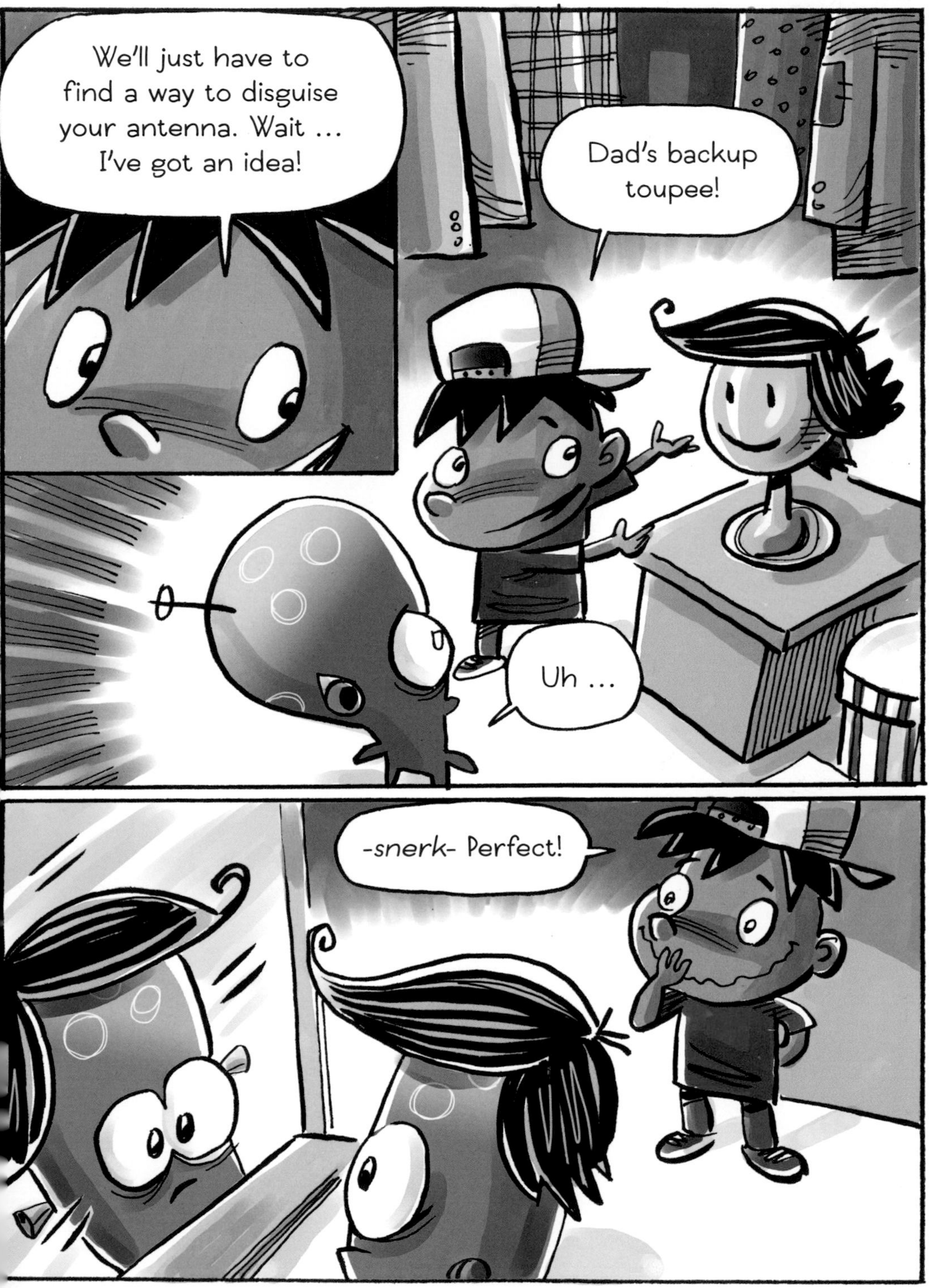
We'll just have to find a way to disguise your antenna. Wait ... I've got an idea!
Dad's backup toupee!
Uh ...
-*snerk*- Perfect!

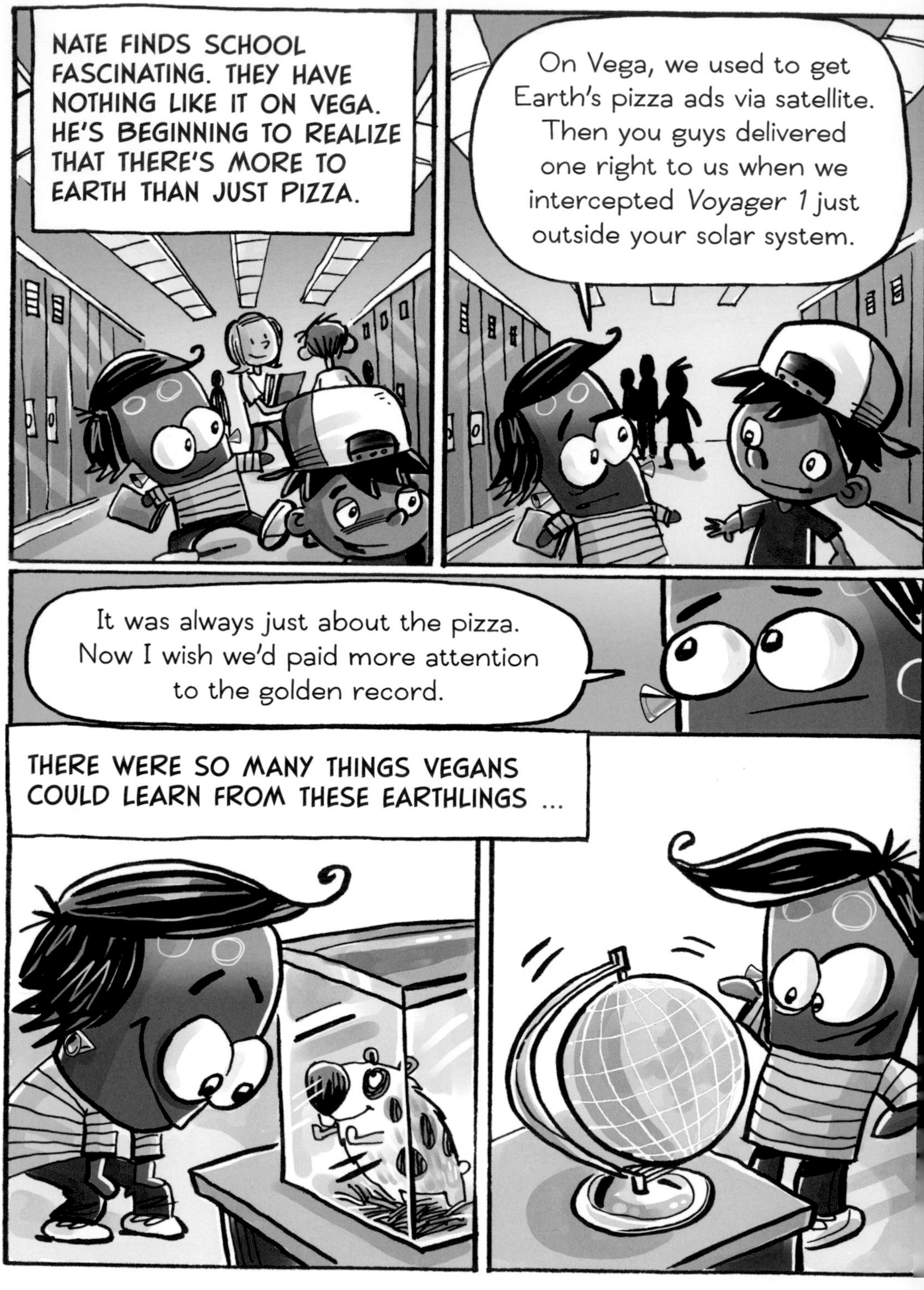
NATE FINDS SCHOOL FASCINATING. THEY HAVE NOTHING LIKE IT ON VEGA. HE'S BEGINNING TO REALIZE THAT THERE'S MORE TO EARTH THAN JUST PIZZA.
On Vega, we used to get Earth's pizza ads via satellite. Then you guys delivered one right to us when we intercepted *Voyager 1* just outside your solar system.
It was always just about the pizza. Now I wish we'd paid more attention to the golden record.
THERE WERE SO MANY THINGS VEGANS COULD LEARN FROM THESE EARTHLINGS ...

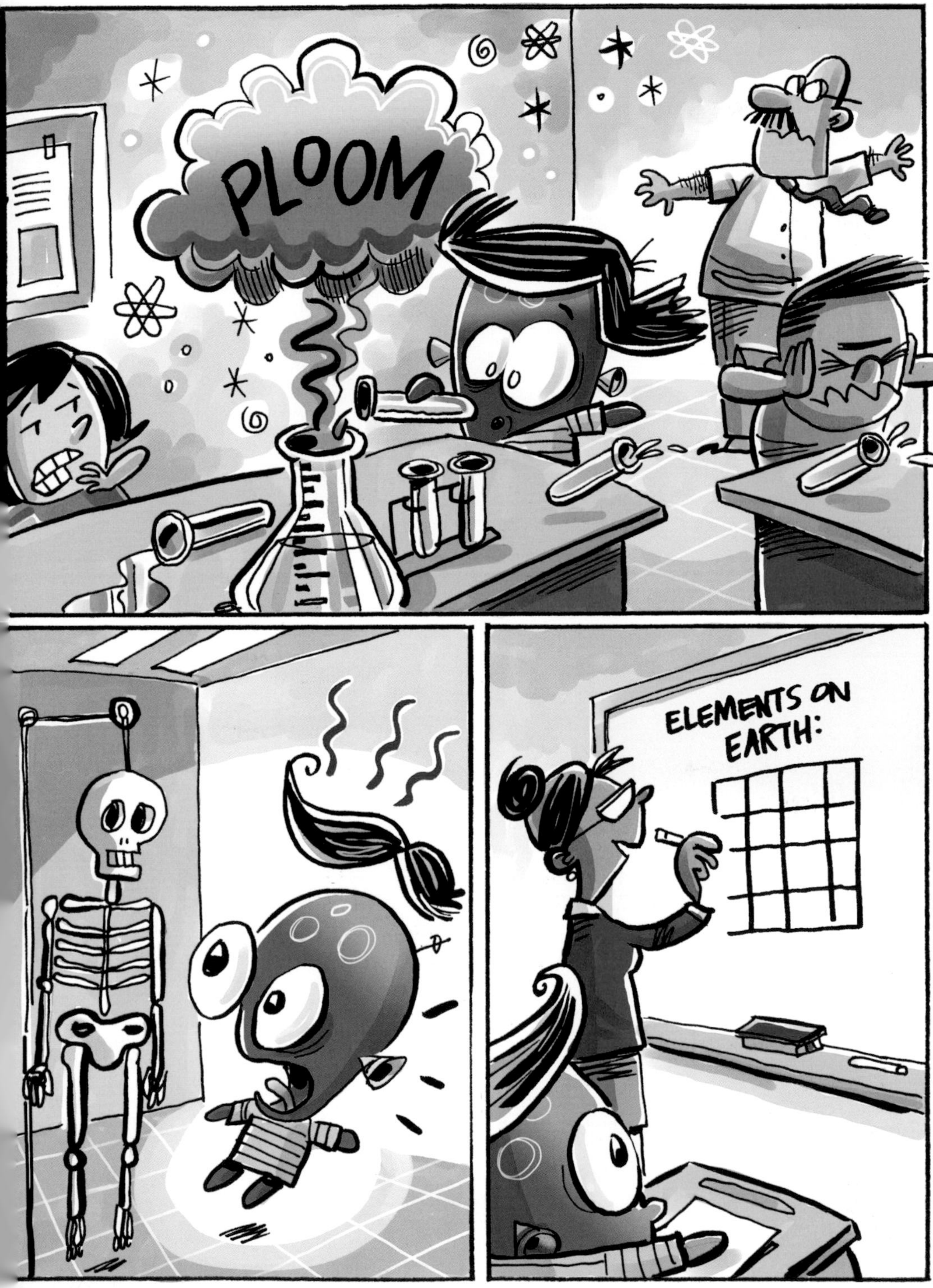
PLOOM
ELEMENTS ON EARTH:

What is this strange thing?
It's a book!
FLIP
FLIP
FLIP
SNIIIIIIFF
What do I plug it into?
Um ... your mind.

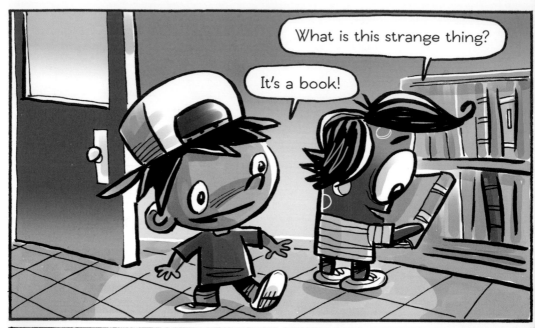

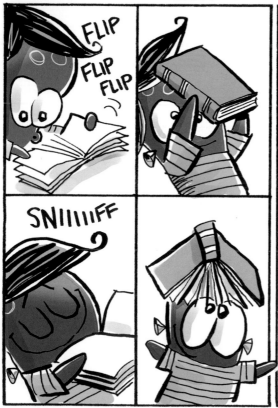

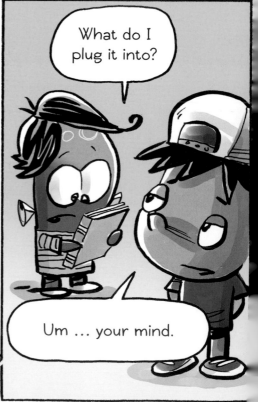

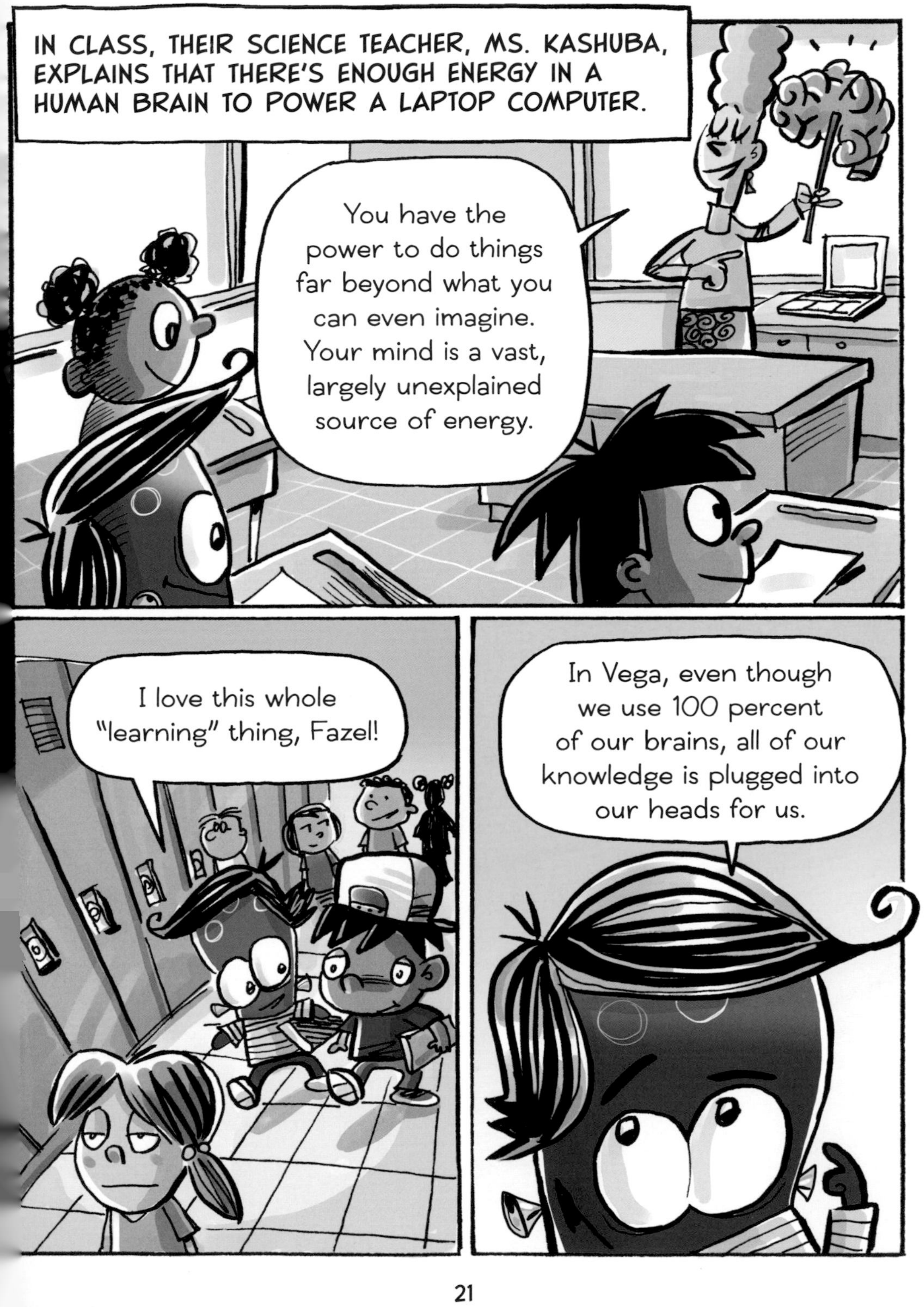
IN CLASS, THEIR SCIENCE TEACHER, MS. KASHUBA, EXPLAINS THAT THERE'S ENOUGH ENERGY IN A HUMAN BRAIN TO POWER A LAPTOP COMPUTER.
You have the power to do things far beyond what you can even imagine. Your mind is a vast, largely unexplained source of energy.
I love this whole "learning" thing, Fazel!
In Vega, even though we use 100 percent of our brains, all of our knowledge is plugged into our heads for us.

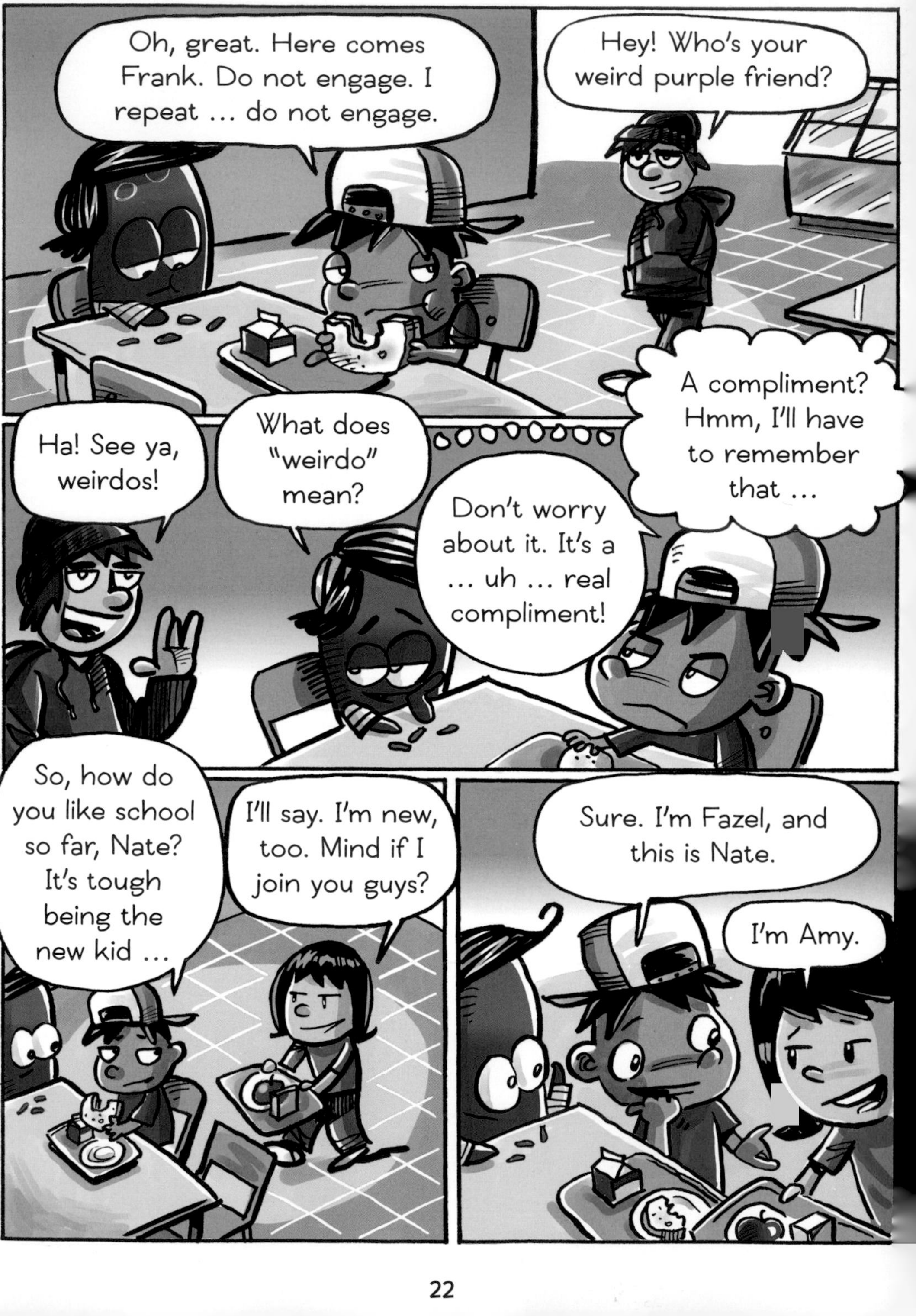
Oh, great. Here comes Frank. Do not engage. I repeat … do not engage.
Hey! Who's your weird purple friend?
Ha! See ya, weirdos!
What does "weirdo" mean?
Don't worry about it. It's a … uh … real compliment!
A compliment? Hmm, I'll have to remember that …
So, how do you like school so far, Nate? It's tough being the new kid …
I'll say. I'm new, too. Mind if I join you guys?
Sure. I'm Fazel, and this is Nate.
I'm Amy.

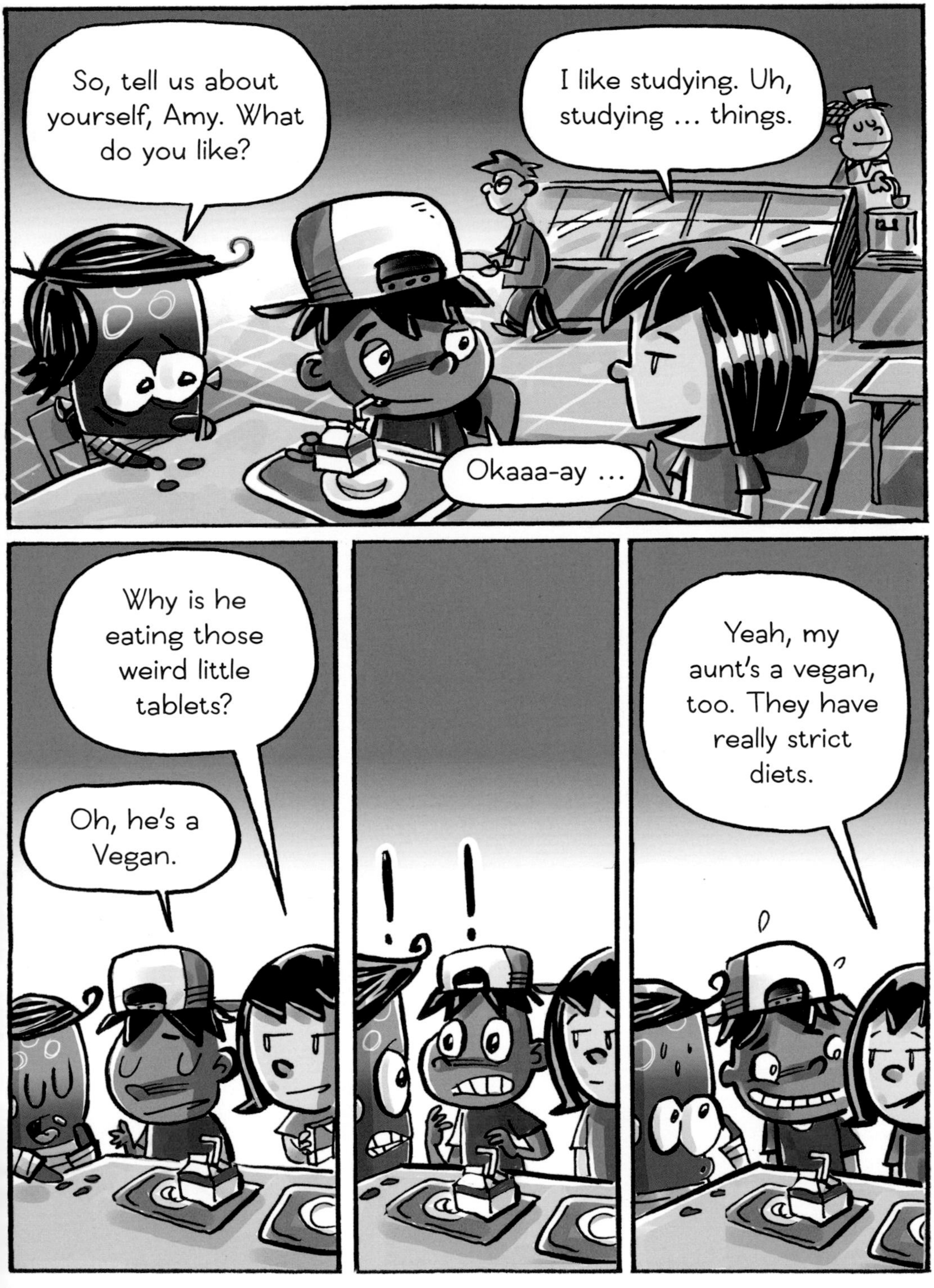
So, tell us about yourself, Amy. What do you like?
I like studying. Uh, studying ... things.
Okaaa-ay ...
Why is he eating those weird little tablets?
Oh, he's a Vegan.
! !
Yeah, my aunt's a vegan, too. They have really strict diets.

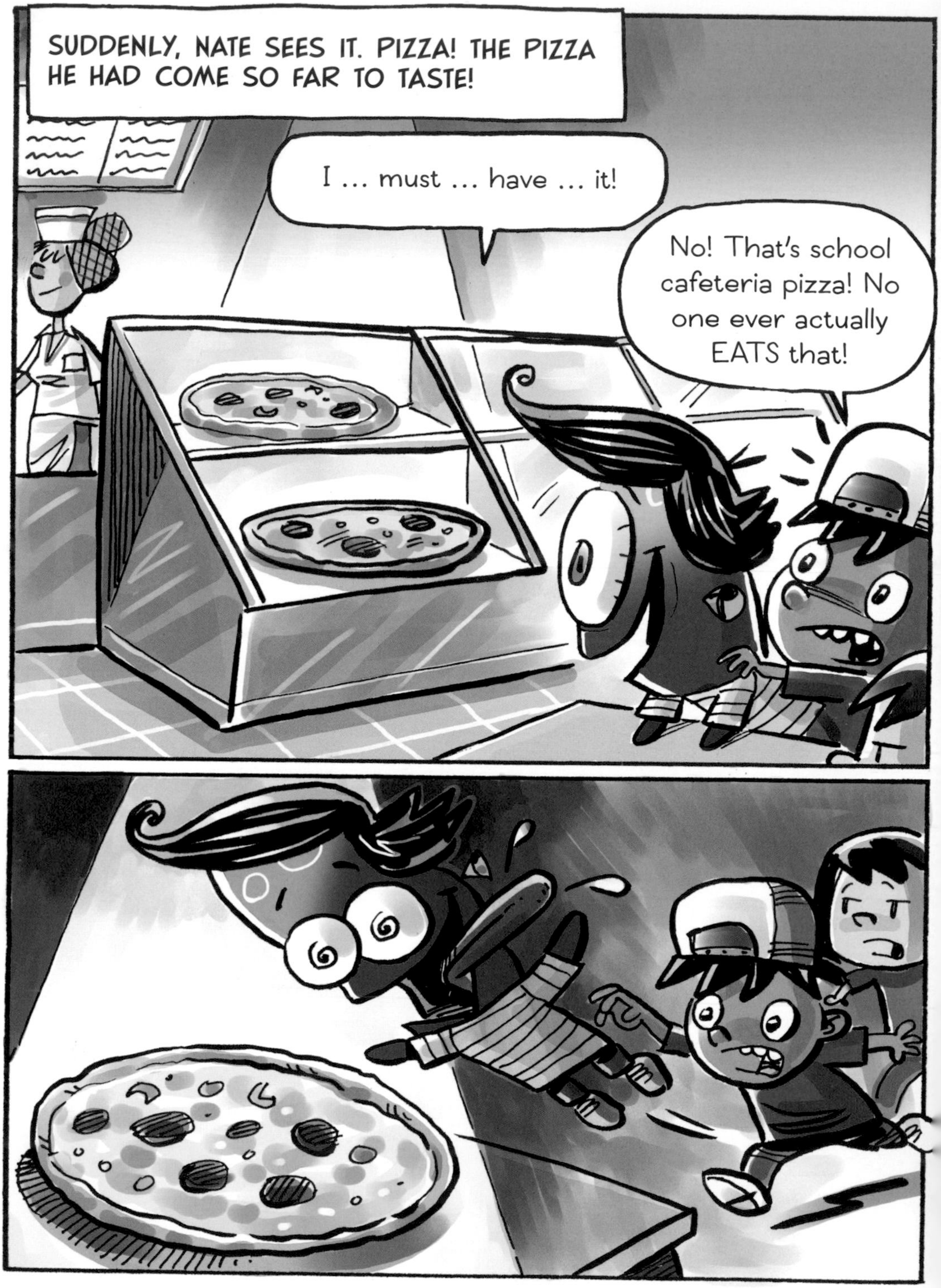
SUDDENLY, NATE SEES IT. PIZZA! THE PIZZA HE HAD COME SO FAR TO TASTE!
I ... must ... have ... it!
No! That's school cafeteria pizza! No one ever actually EATS that!

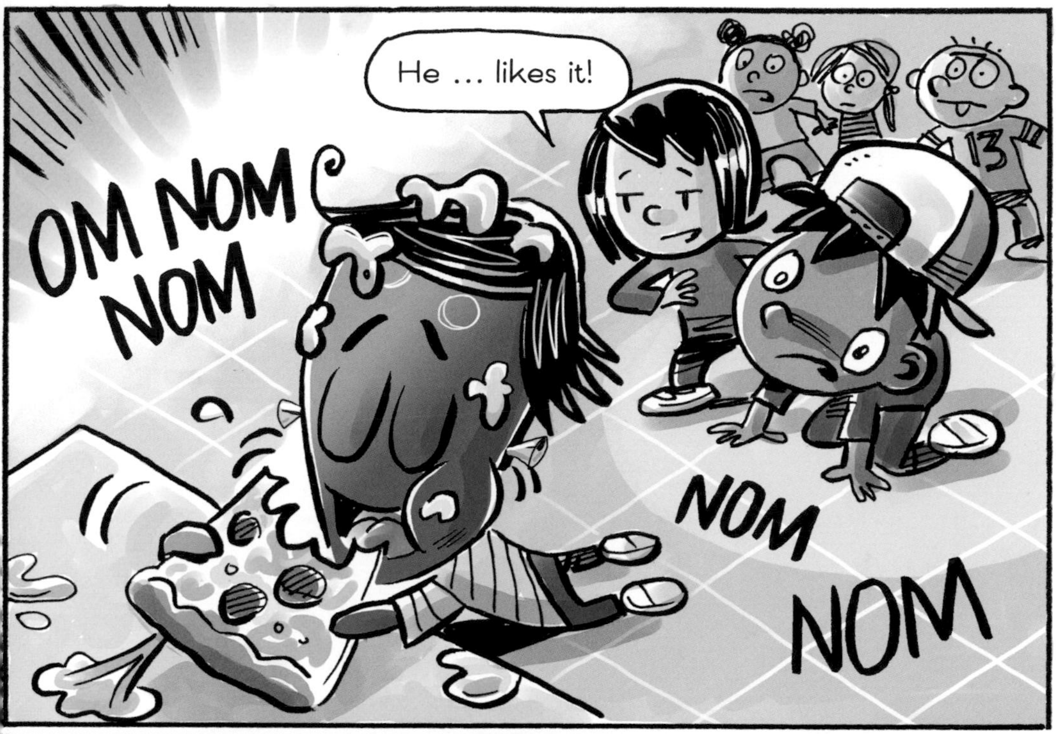
He ... likes it!
OM NOM NOM
NOM NOM

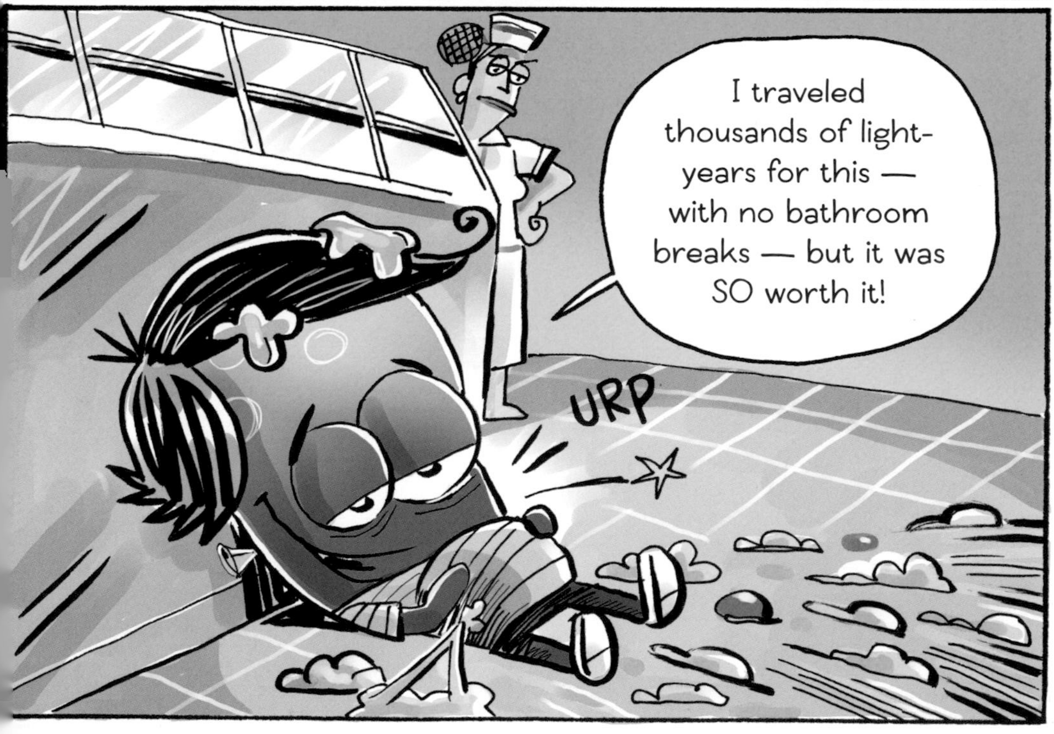
I traveled thousands of light-years for this — with no bathroom breaks — but it was SO worth it!
URP

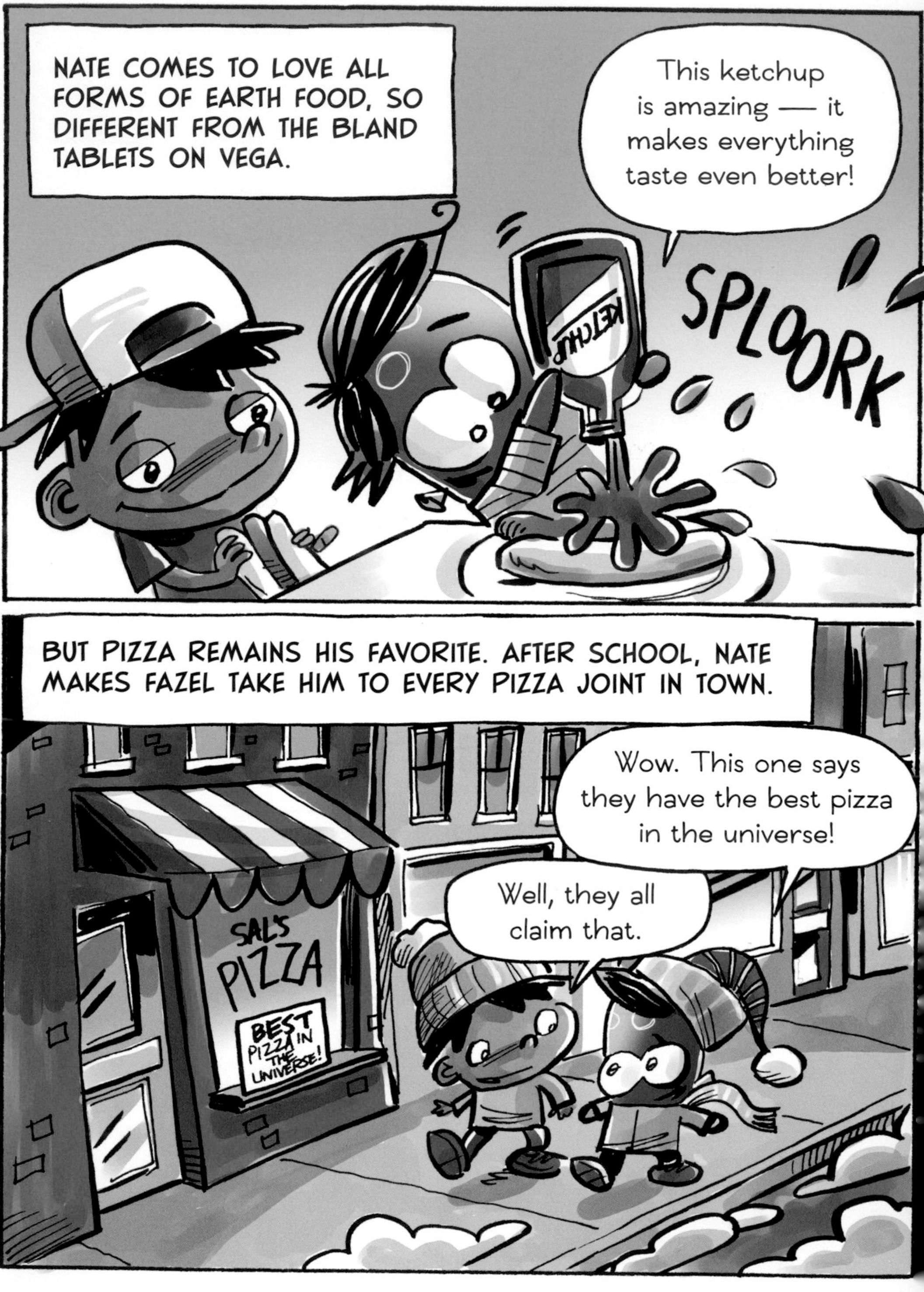
NATE COMES TO LOVE ALL FORMS OF EARTH FOOD, SO DIFFERENT FROM THE BLAND TABLETS ON VEGA.
This ketchup is amazing — it makes everything taste even better!
SPLOORK
KETCHUP
BUT PIZZA REMAINS HIS FAVORITE. AFTER SCHOOL, NATE MAKES FAZEL TAKE HIM TO EVERY PIZZA JOINT IN TOWN.
Wow. This one says they have the best pizza in the universe!
Well, they all claim that.
SAL'S PIZZA
BEST PIZZA IN THE UNIVERSE!

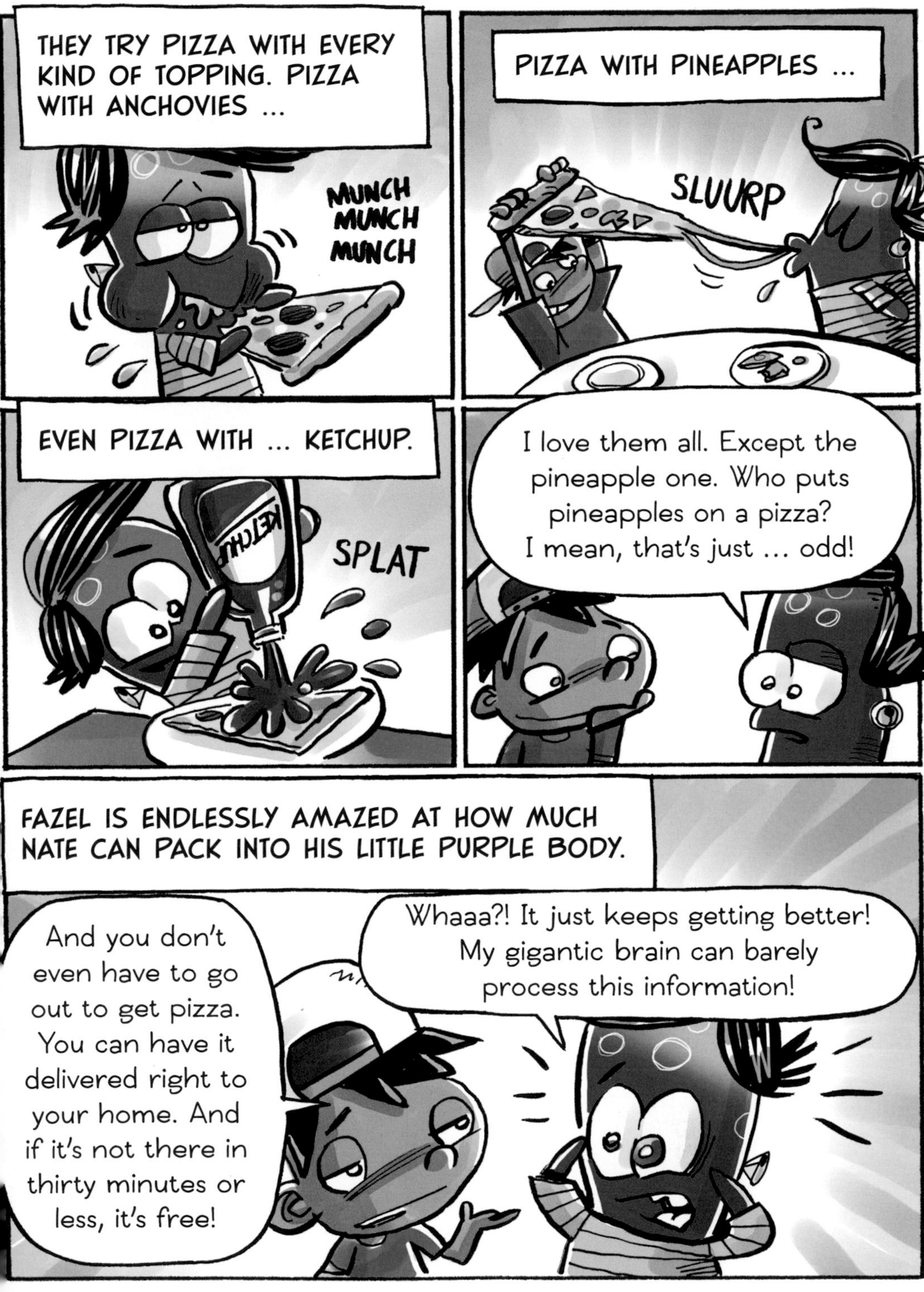
THEY TRY PIZZA WITH EVERY KIND OF TOPPING. PIZZA WITH ANCHOVIES ...
MUNCH MUNCH MUNCH
PIZZA WITH PINEAPPLES ...
SLUURP
EVEN PIZZA WITH ... KETCHUP.
KETCHUP
SPLAT
I love them all. Except the pineapple one. Who puts pineapples on a pizza? I mean, that's just ... odd!
FAZEL IS ENDLESSLY AMAZED AT HOW MUCH NATE CAN PACK INTO HIS LITTLE PURPLE BODY.
And you don't even have to go out to get pizza. You can have it delivered right to your home. And if it's not there in thirty minutes or less, it's free!
Whaaa?! It just keeps getting better! My gigantic brain can barely process this information!

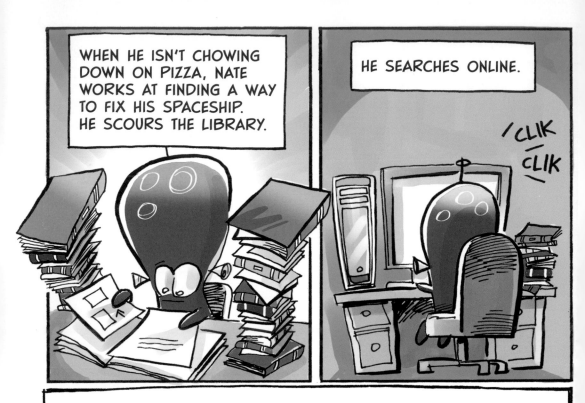

WHEN HE ISN'T CHOWING DOWN ON PIZZA, NATE WORKS AT FINDING A WAY TO FIX HIS SPACESHIP. HE SCOURS THE LIBRARY.

HE SEARCHES ONLINE.

CLIK CLIK

BUT OF COURSE HE CAN'T FIND ANY INFORMATION ON EARTH ABOUT HOW TO REPAIR A VEGAN SPACESHIP. IT'S LIKE BEING TRAPPED ON PLANET ZOGTAR WITHOUT A ZORGBLATT!

Did you try googling "How to repair a Vegan spaceship"?

Yeah, and believe it or not, a lot of stuff came up ... but nothing helpful.

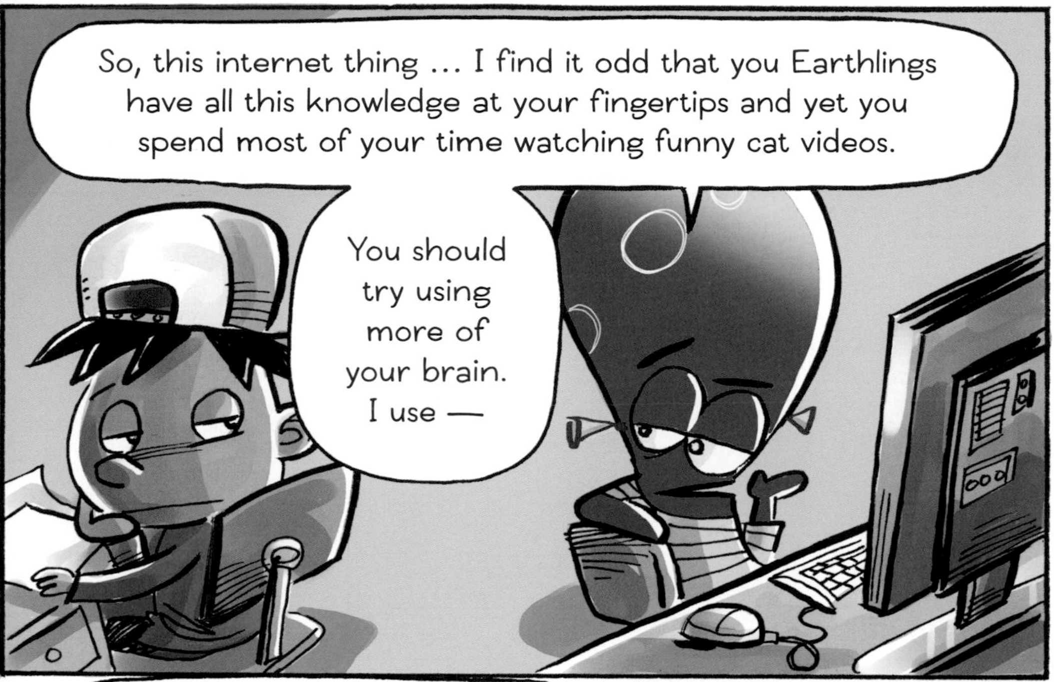
So, this internet thing ... I find it odd that you Earthlings have all this knowledge at your fingertips and yet you spend most of your time watching funny cat videos.
You should try using more of your brain. I use —

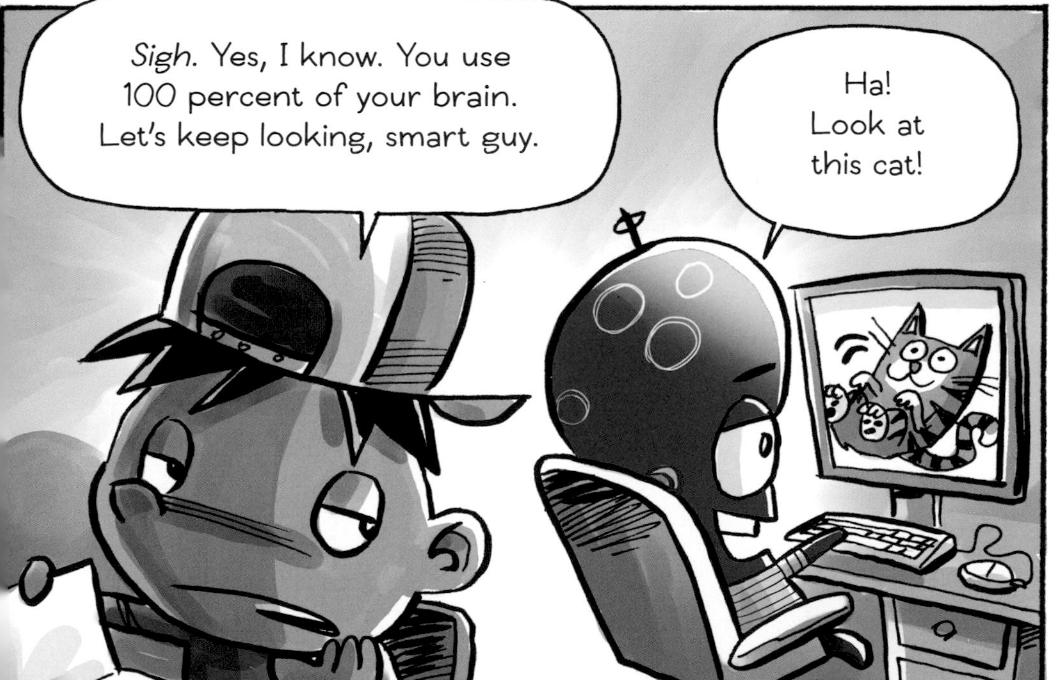
Sigh. Yes, I know. You use 100 percent of your brain. Let's keep looking, smart guy.
Ha! Look at this cat!

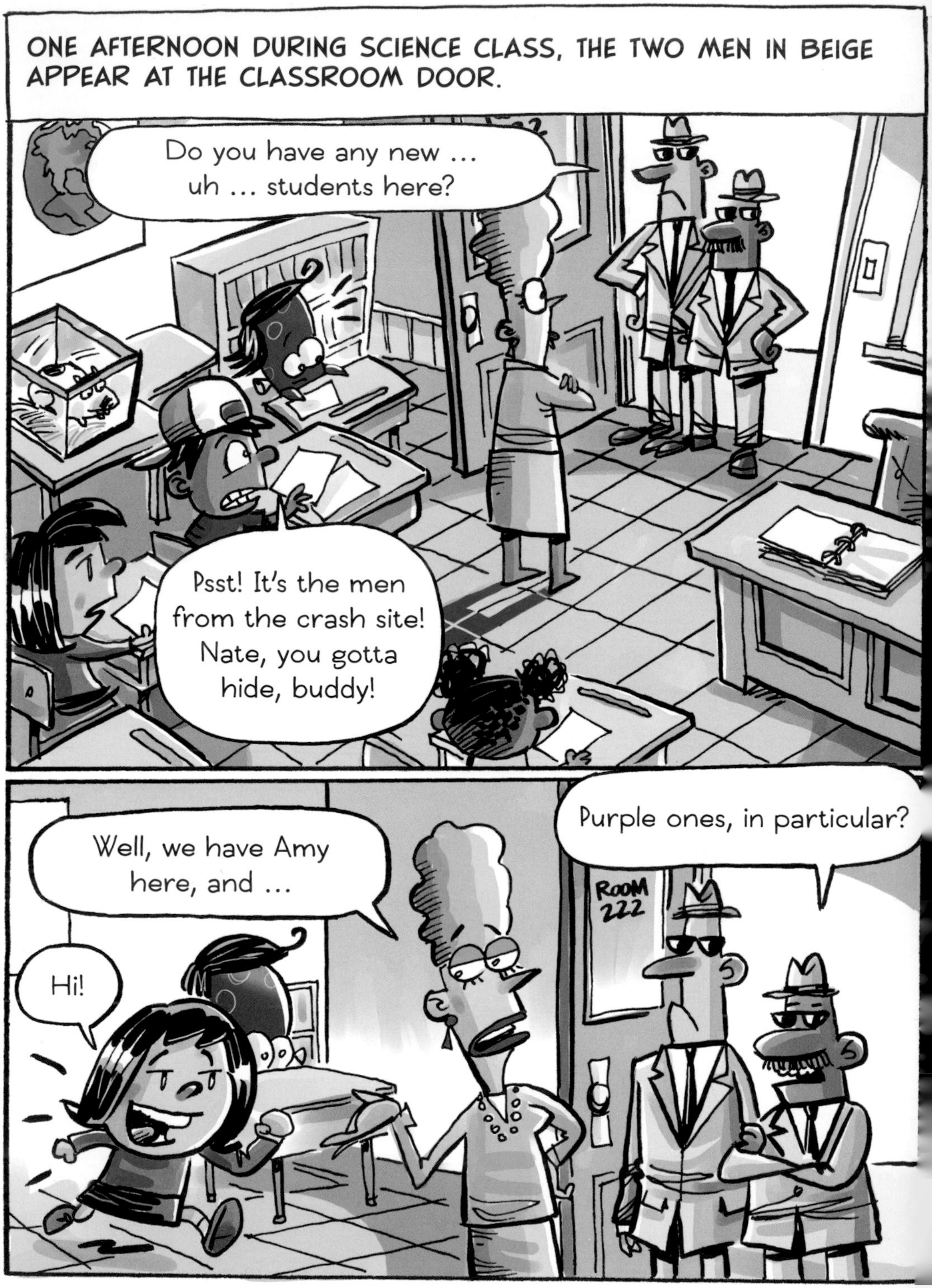
ONE AFTERNOON DURING SCIENCE CLASS, THE TWO MEN IN BEIGE APPEAR AT THE CLASSROOM DOOR.
Do you have any new … uh … students here?
Psst! It's the men from the crash site! Nate, you gotta hide, buddy!
Well, we have Amy here, and …
Hi!
ROOM 222
Purple ones, in particular?

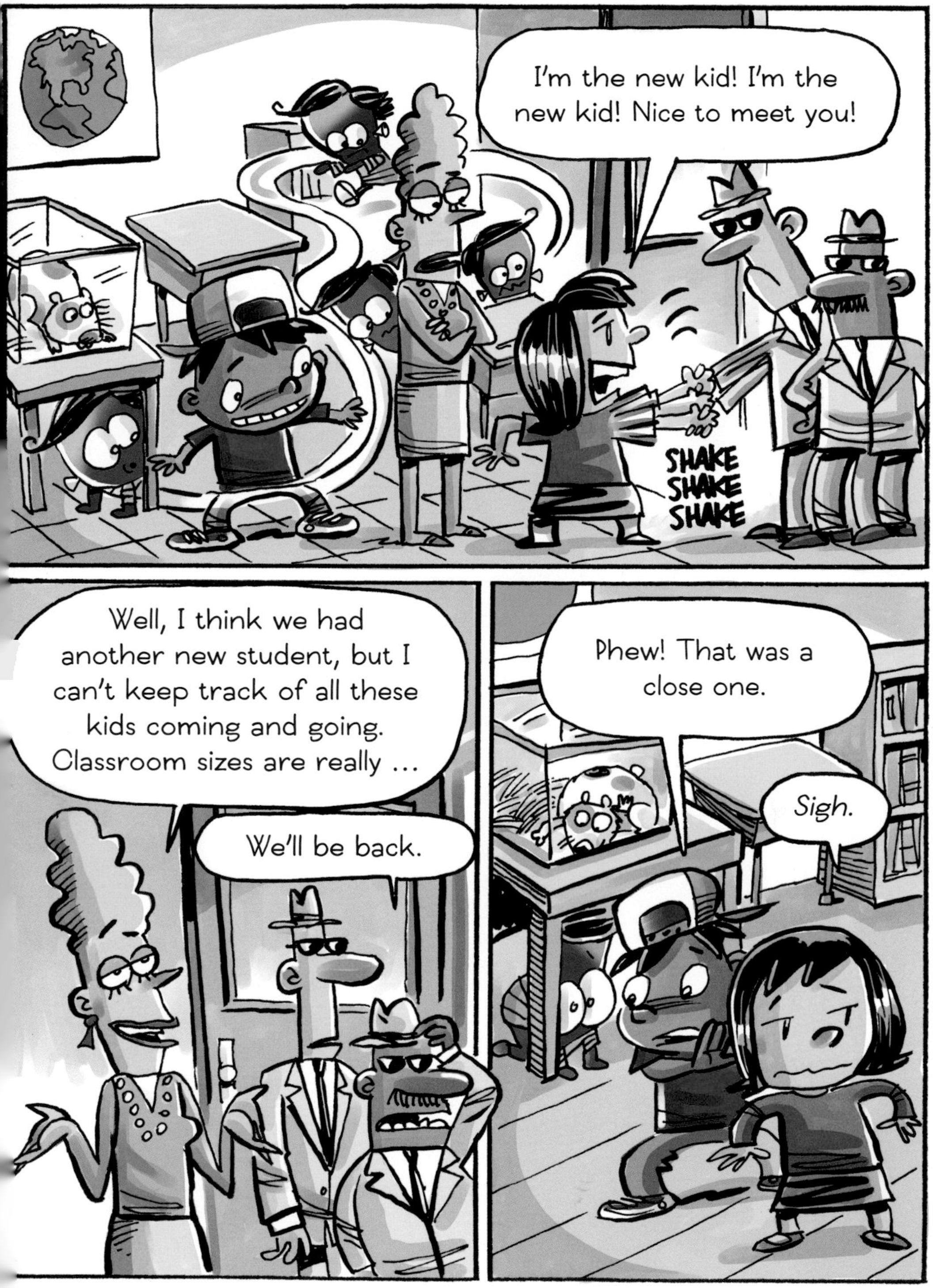
I'm the new kid! I'm the new kid! Nice to meet you!
SHAKE SHAKE SHAKE
Well, I think we had another new student, but I can't keep track of all these kids coming and going. Classroom sizes are really …
We'll be back.
Phew! That was a close one.
Sigh.

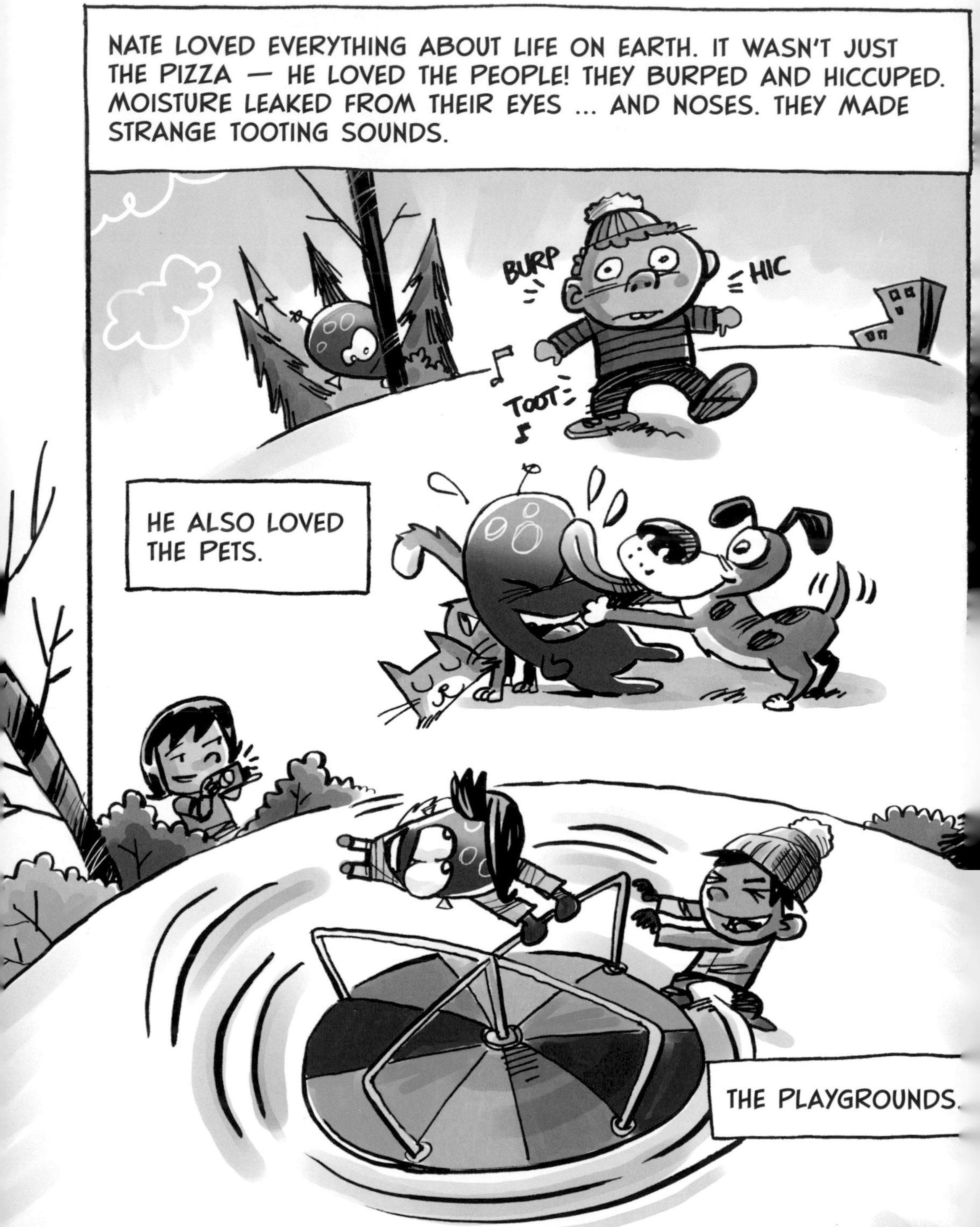
NATE LOVED EVERYTHING ABOUT LIFE ON EARTH. IT WASN'T JUST THE PIZZA — HE LOVED THE PEOPLE! THEY BURPED AND HICCUPED. MOISTURE LEAKED FROM THEIR EYES ... AND NOSES. THEY MADE STRANGE TOOTING SOUNDS.
BURP
HIC
TOOT
HE ALSO LOVED THE PETS.
THE PLAYGROUNDS.

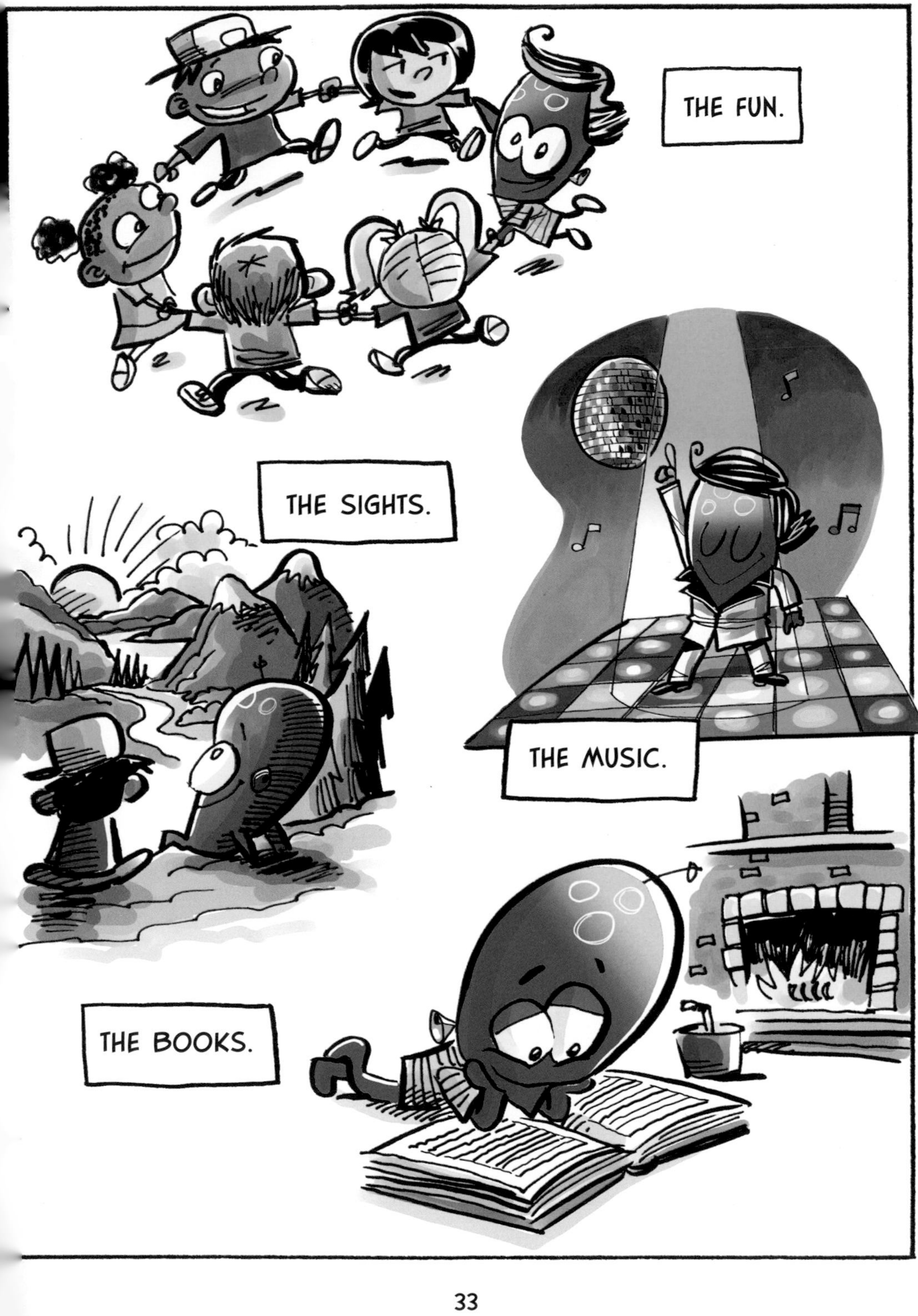
THE FUN.
THE SIGHTS.
THE MUSIC.
THE BOOKS.

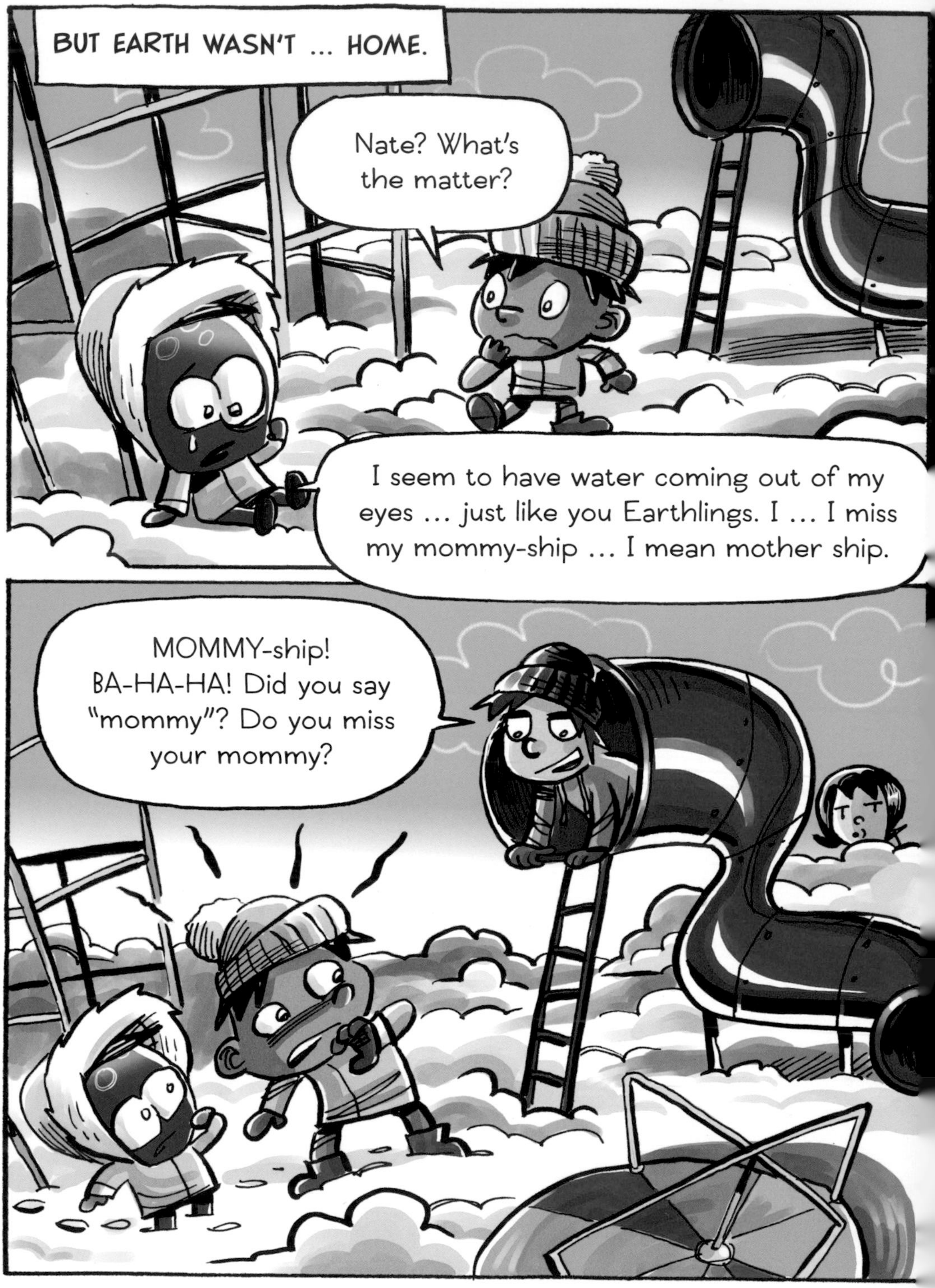
BUT EARTH WASN'T ... HOME.
Nate? What's the matter?
I seem to have water coming out of my eyes ... just like you Earthlings. I ... I miss my mommy-ship ... I mean mother ship.
MOMMY-ship! BA-HA-HA! Did you say "mommy"? Do you miss your mommy?

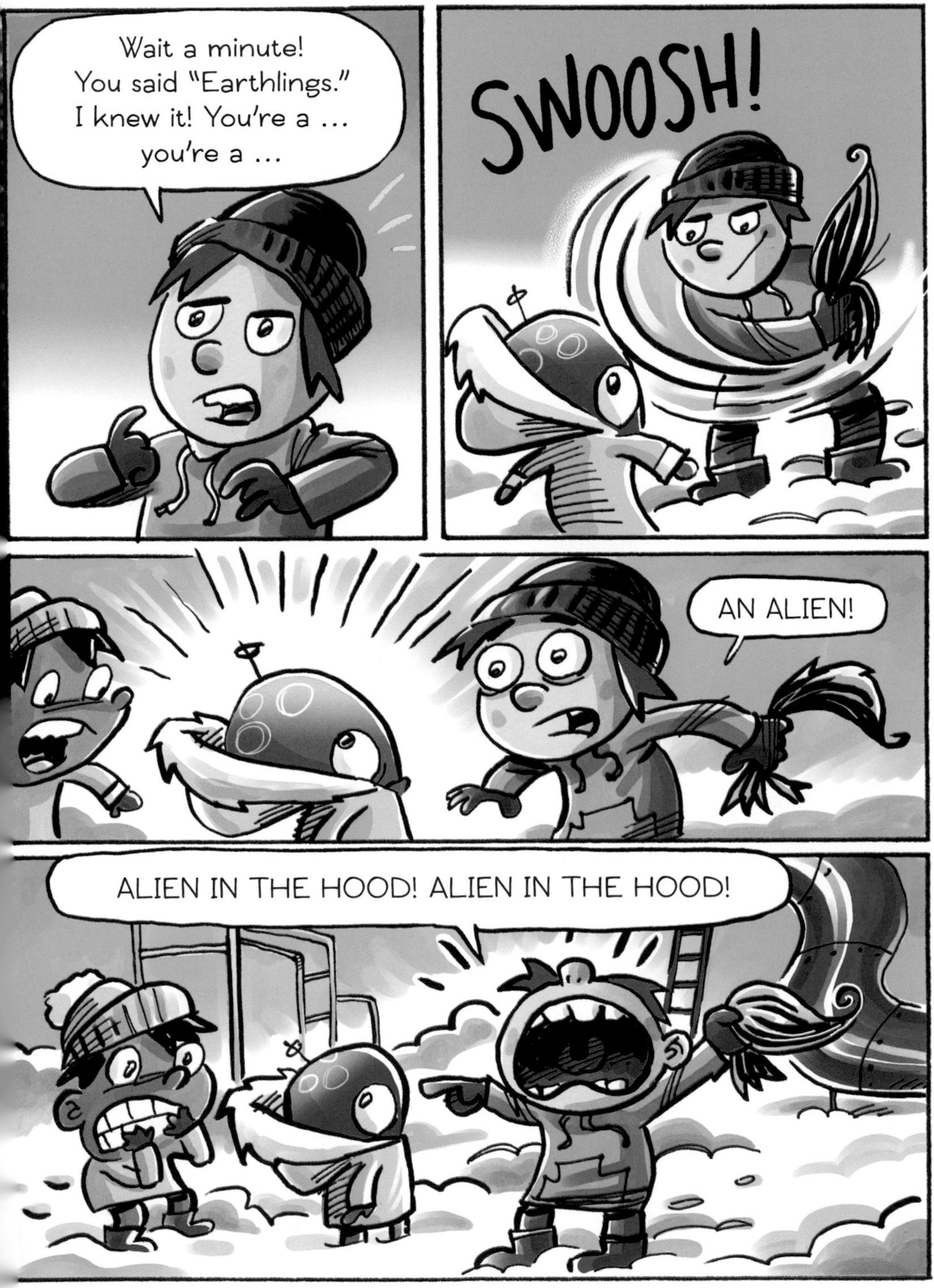

Wait a minute! You said "Earthlings." I knew it! You're a ... you're a ...
SWOOSH!
AN ALIEN!
ALIEN IN THE HOOD! ALIEN IN THE HOOD!

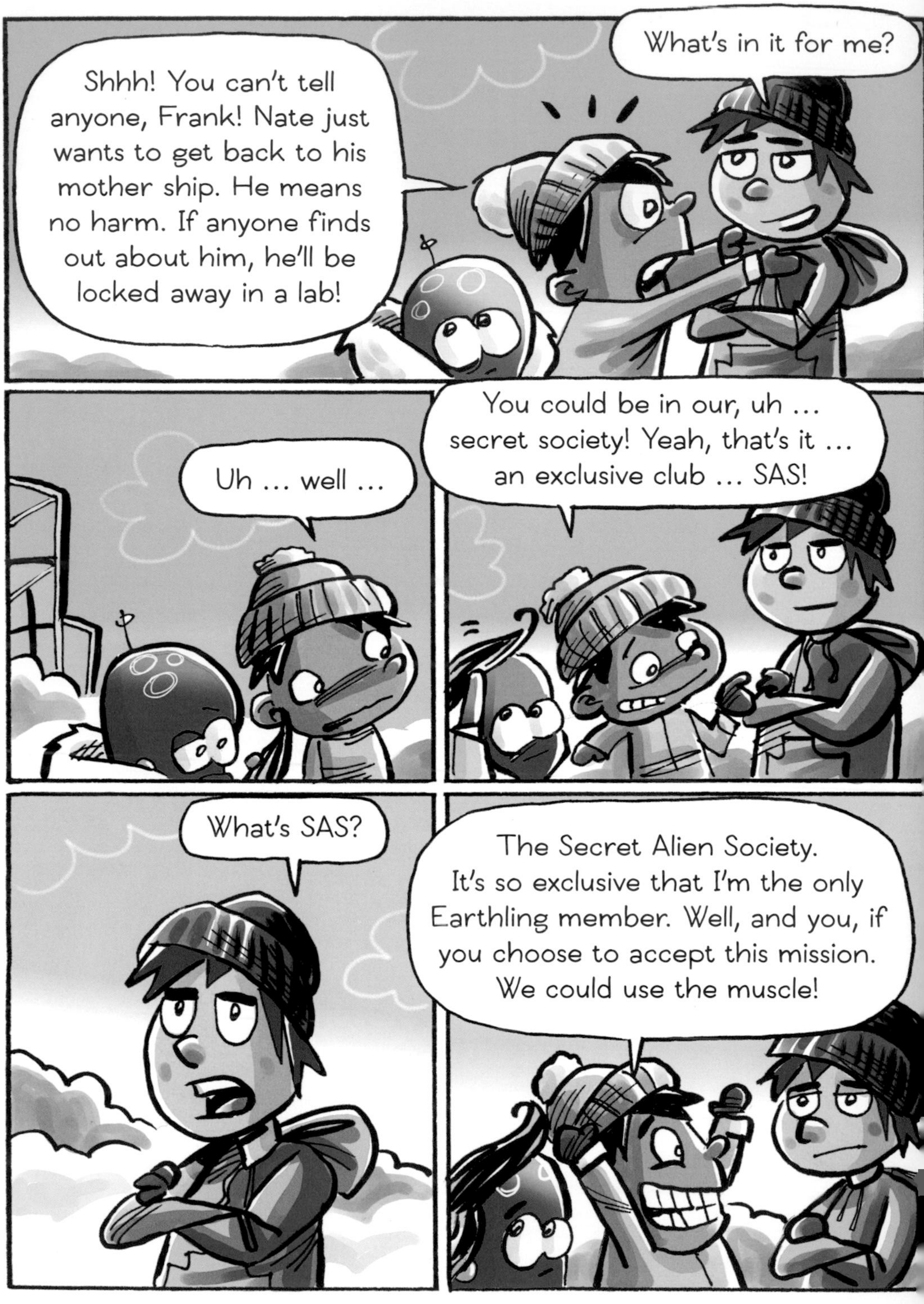
What's in it for me?
Shhh! You can't tell anyone, Frank! Nate just wants to get back to his mother ship. He means no harm. If anyone finds out about him, he'll be locked away in a lab!
Uh ... well ...
You could be in our, uh ... secret society! Yeah, that's it ... an exclusive club ... SAS!
What's SAS?
The Secret Alien Society. It's so exclusive that I'm the only Earthling member. Well, and you, if you choose to accept this mission. We could use the muscle!

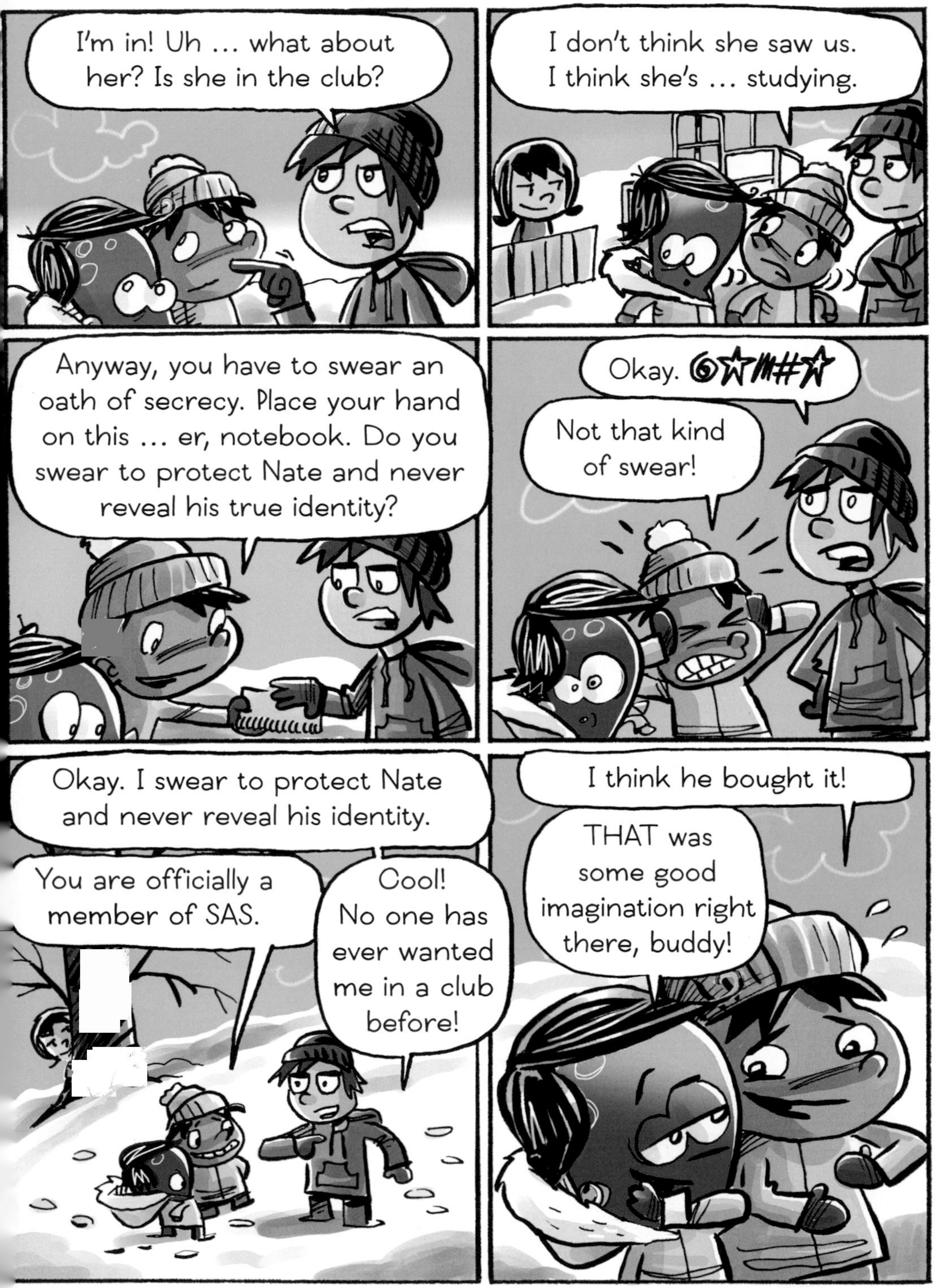
I'm in! Uh ... what about her? Is she in the club?
I don't think she saw us. I think she's ... studying.
Anyway, you have to swear an oath of secrecy. Place your hand on this ... er, notebook. Do you swear to protect Nate and never reveal his true identity?
Okay.
Not that kind of swear!
Okay. I swear to protect Nate and never reveal his identity.
You are officially a member of SAS.
Cool! No one has ever wanted me in a club before!
I think he bought it!
THAT was some good imagination right there, buddy!

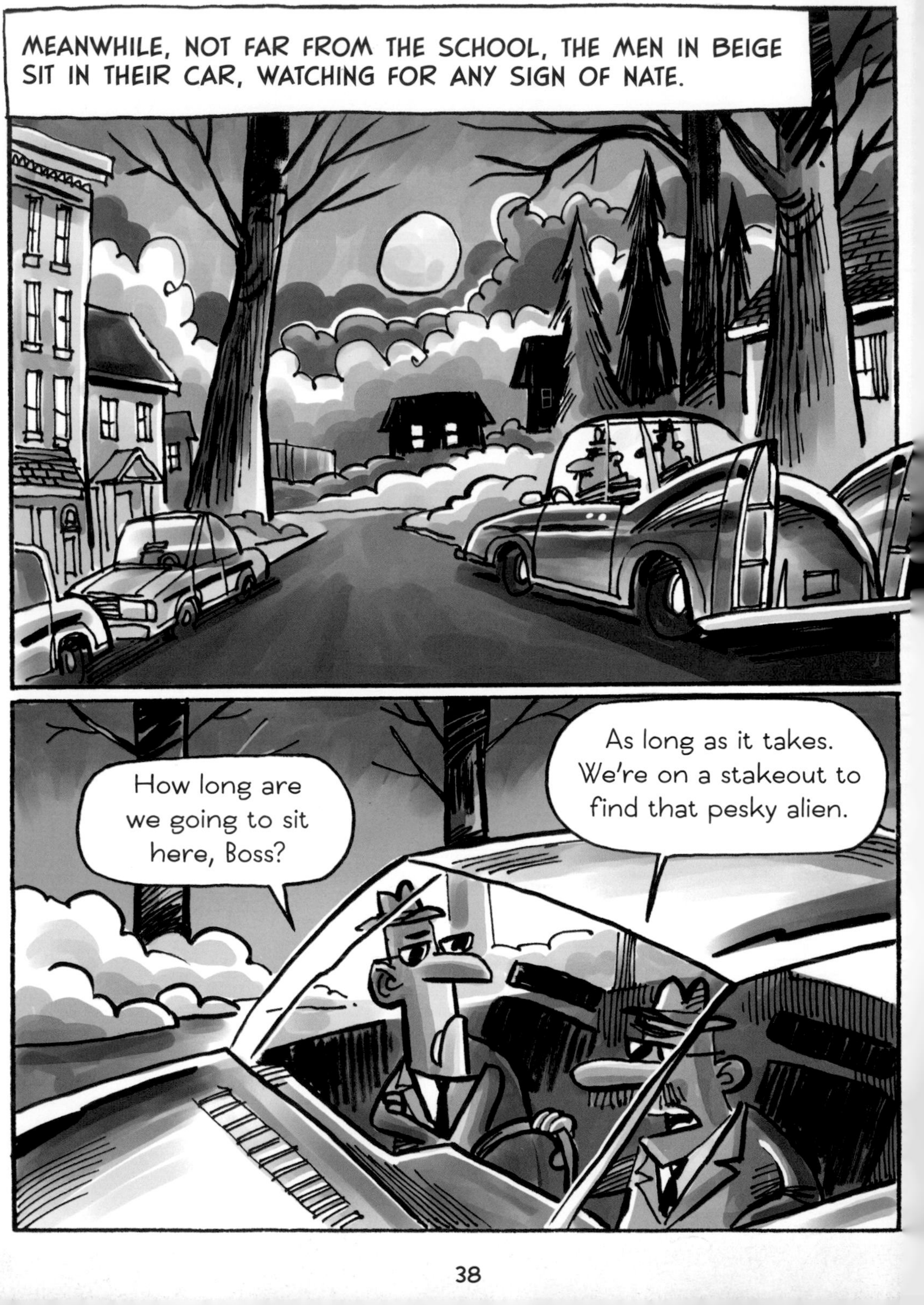
MEANWHILE, NOT FAR FROM THE SCHOOL, THE MEN IN BEIGE SIT IN THEIR CAR, WATCHING FOR ANY SIGN OF NATE.
How long are we going to sit here, Boss?
As long as it takes. We're on a stakeout to find that pesky alien.

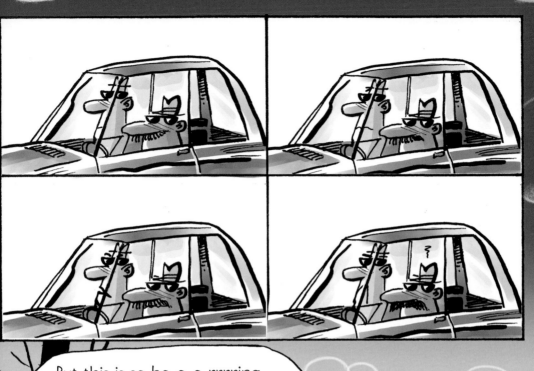

But this is so bo-o-o-rrrring. On TV shows, they always have snacks when they do a stakeout. Can we at least get some pizza to pass the time ...?

Oh, for cryin' out loud! Okay, we'll get some pizza!

Also ... I have to pee again.

Didn't I tell you not to drink all that coffee?

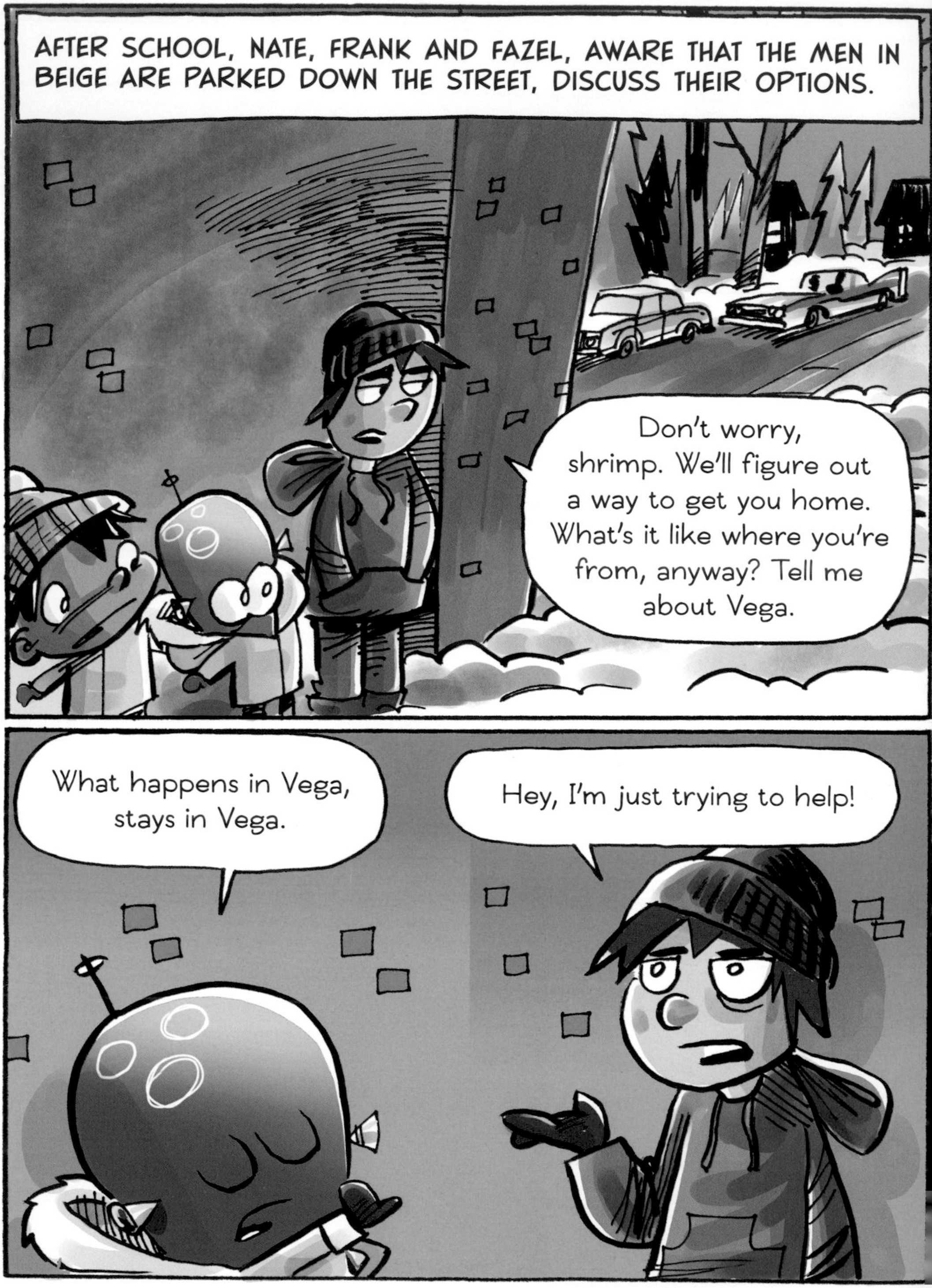
AFTER SCHOOL, NATE, FRANK AND FAZEL, AWARE THAT THE MEN IN BEIGE ARE PARKED DOWN THE STREET, DISCUSS THEIR OPTIONS.
Don't worry, shrimp. We'll figure out a way to get you home. What's it like where you're from, anyway? Tell me about Vega.
What happens in Vega, stays in Vega.
Hey, I'm just trying to help!

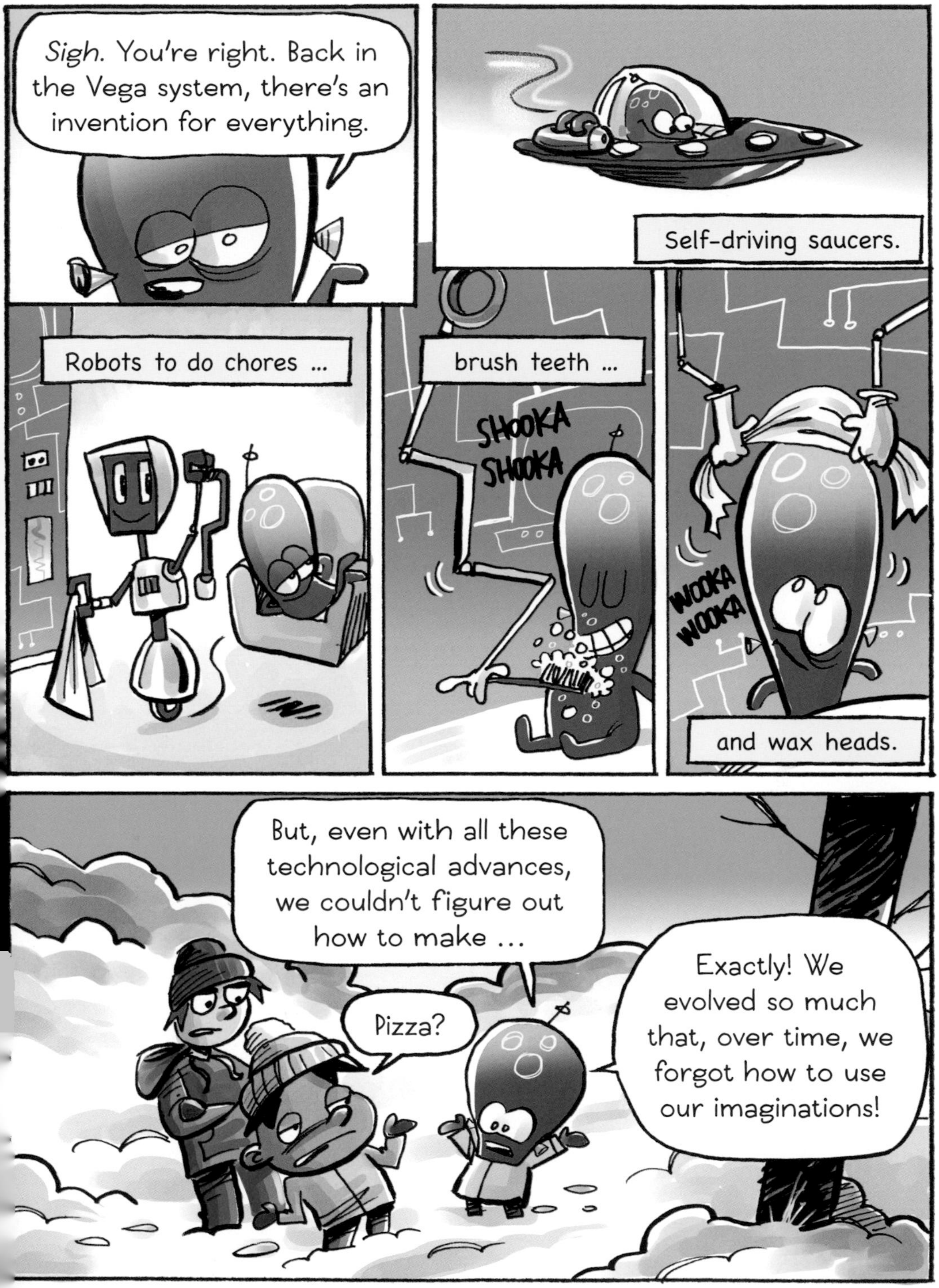
Sigh. You're right. Back in the Vega system, there's an invention for everything.
Self-driving saucers.
Robots to do chores ...
brush teeth ...
SHOOKA SHOOKA
WOOKA WOOKA
and wax heads.
But, even with all these technological advances, we couldn't figure out how to make ...
Pizza?
Exactly! We evolved so much that, over time, we forgot how to use our imaginations!

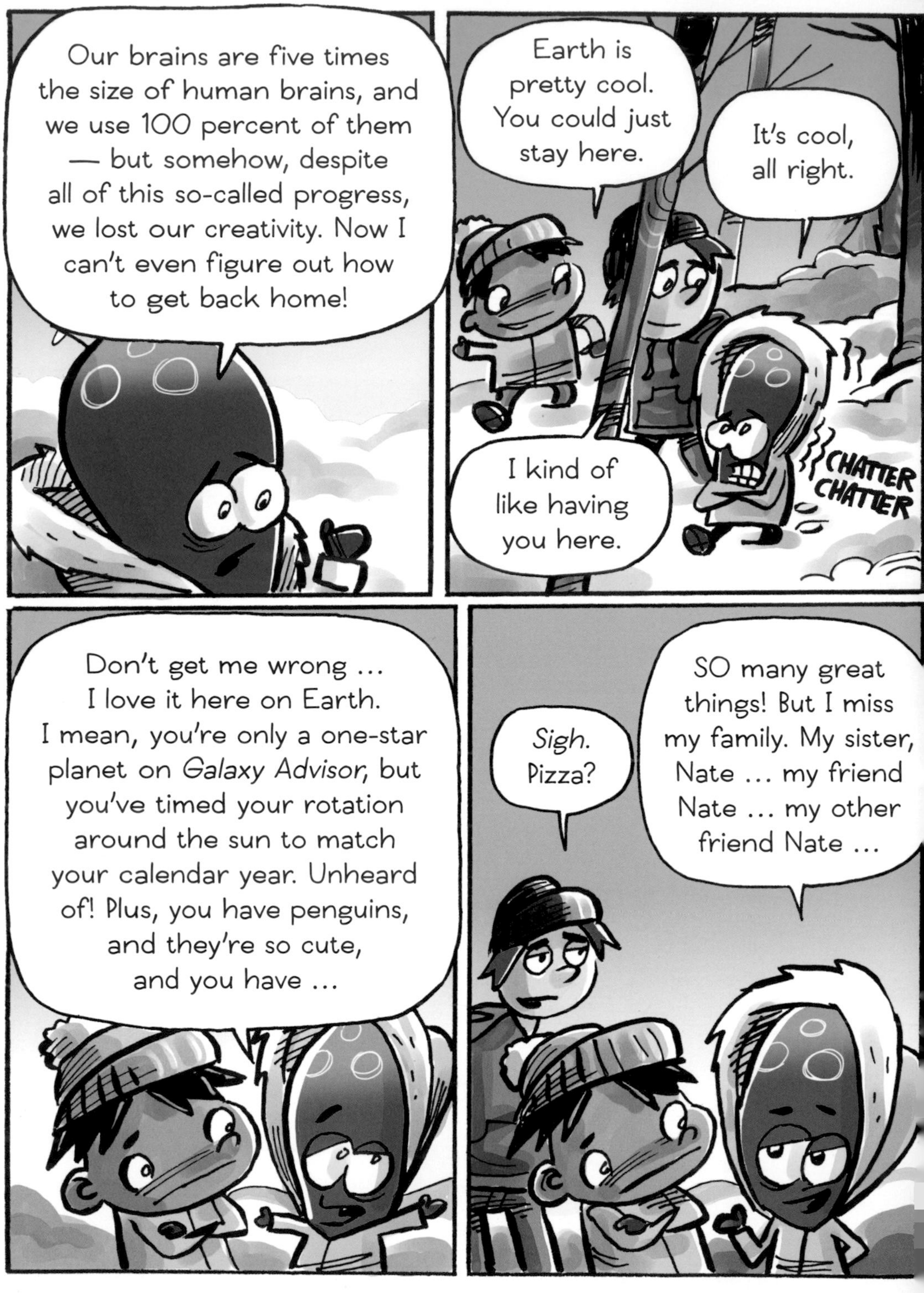
Our brains are five times the size of human brains, and we use 100 percent of them — but somehow, despite all of this so-called progress, we lost our creativity. Now I can't even figure out how to get back home!
Earth is pretty cool. You could just stay here.
It's cool, all right.
I kind of like having you here.
CHATTER CHATTER
Don't get me wrong ... I love it here on Earth. I mean, you're only a one-star planet on *Galaxy Advisor*, but you've timed your rotation around the sun to match your calendar year. Unheard of! Plus, you have penguins, and they're so cute, and you have ...
Sigh. Pizza?
SO many great things! But I miss my family. My sister, Nate ... my friend Nate ... my other friend Nate ...

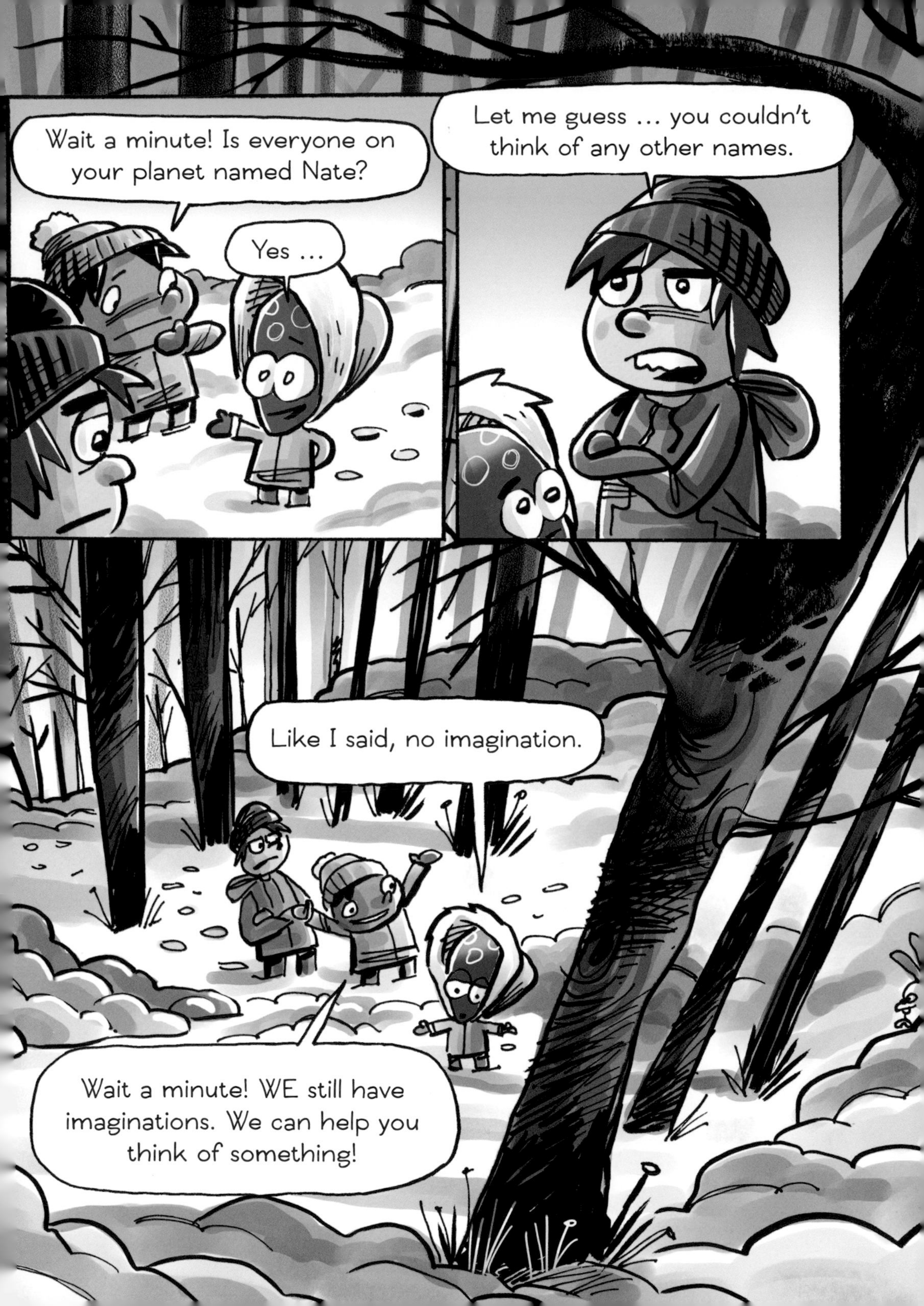
Wait a minute! Is everyone on your planet named Nate?
Yes ...
Let me guess ... you couldn't think of any other names.
Like I said, no imagination.
Wait a minute! WE still have imaginations. We can help you think of something!

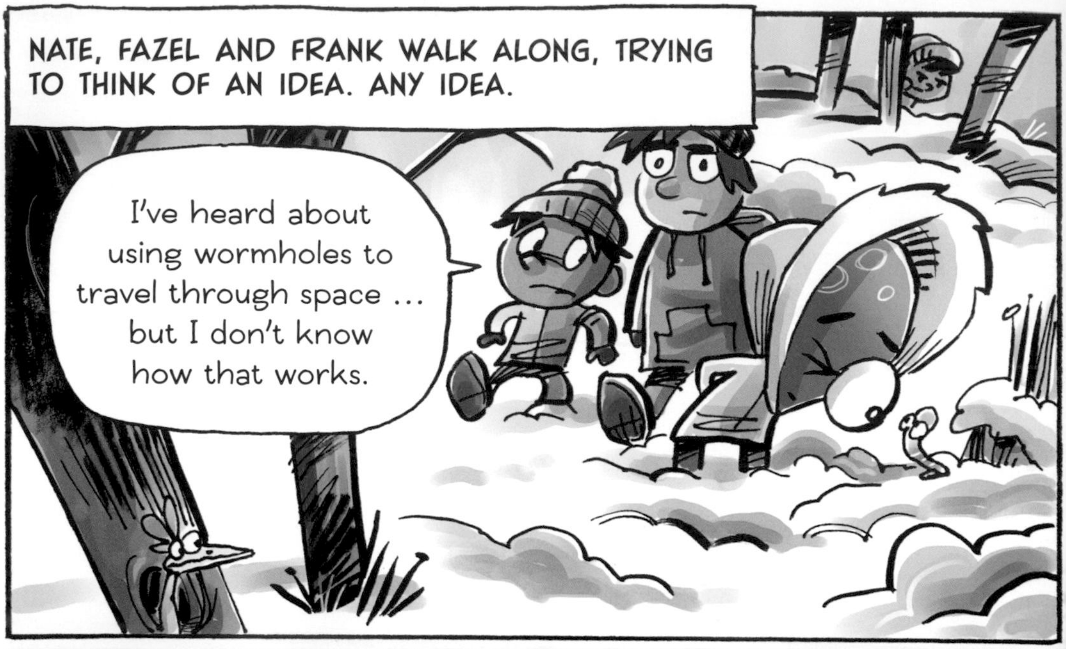
NATE, FAZEL AND FRANK WALK ALONG, TRYING TO THINK OF AN IDEA. ANY IDEA.
I've heard about using wormholes to travel through space ... but I don't know how that works.

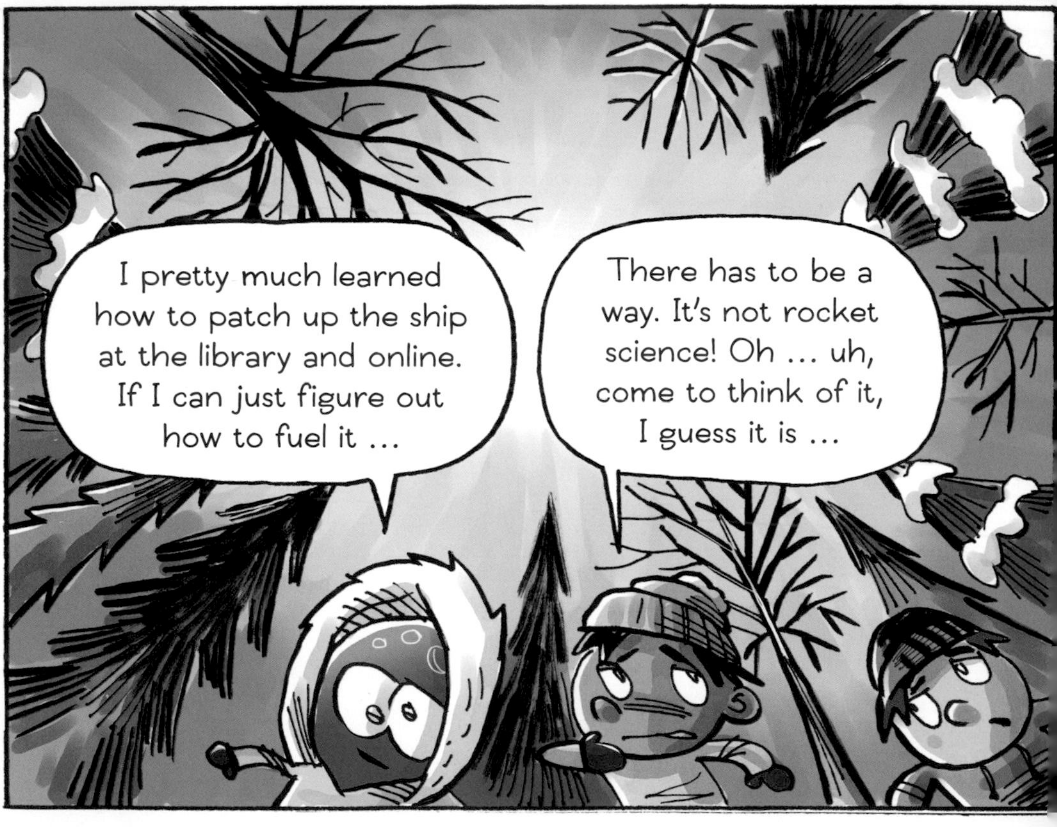
I pretty much learned how to patch up the ship at the library and online. If I can just figure out how to fuel it ...
There has to be a way. It's not rocket science! Oh ... uh, come to think of it, I guess it is ...

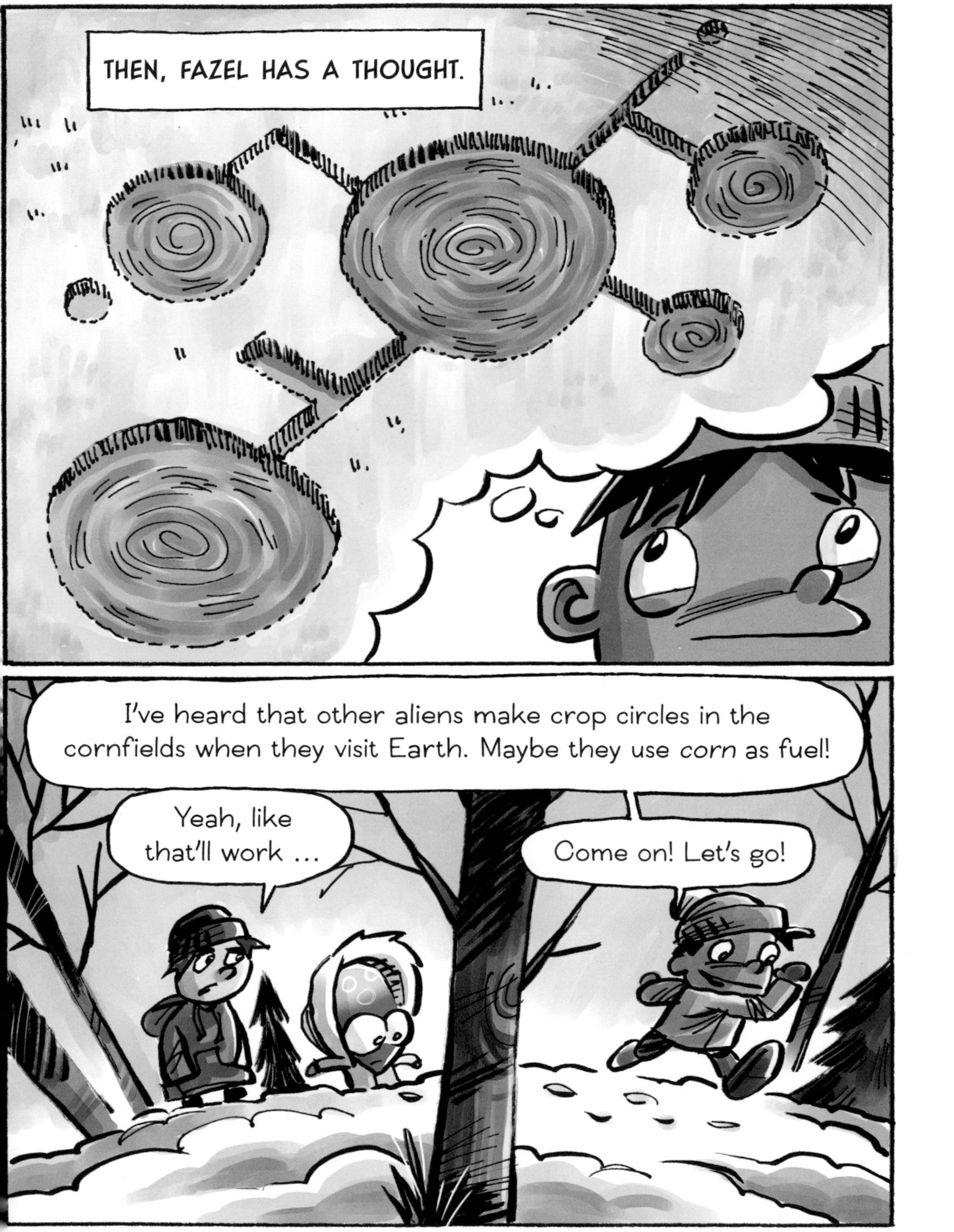
THEN, FAZEL HAS A THOUGHT.
I've heard that other aliens make crop circles in the cornfields when they visit Earth. Maybe they use *corn* as fuel!
Yeah, like that'll work ...
Come on! Let's go!

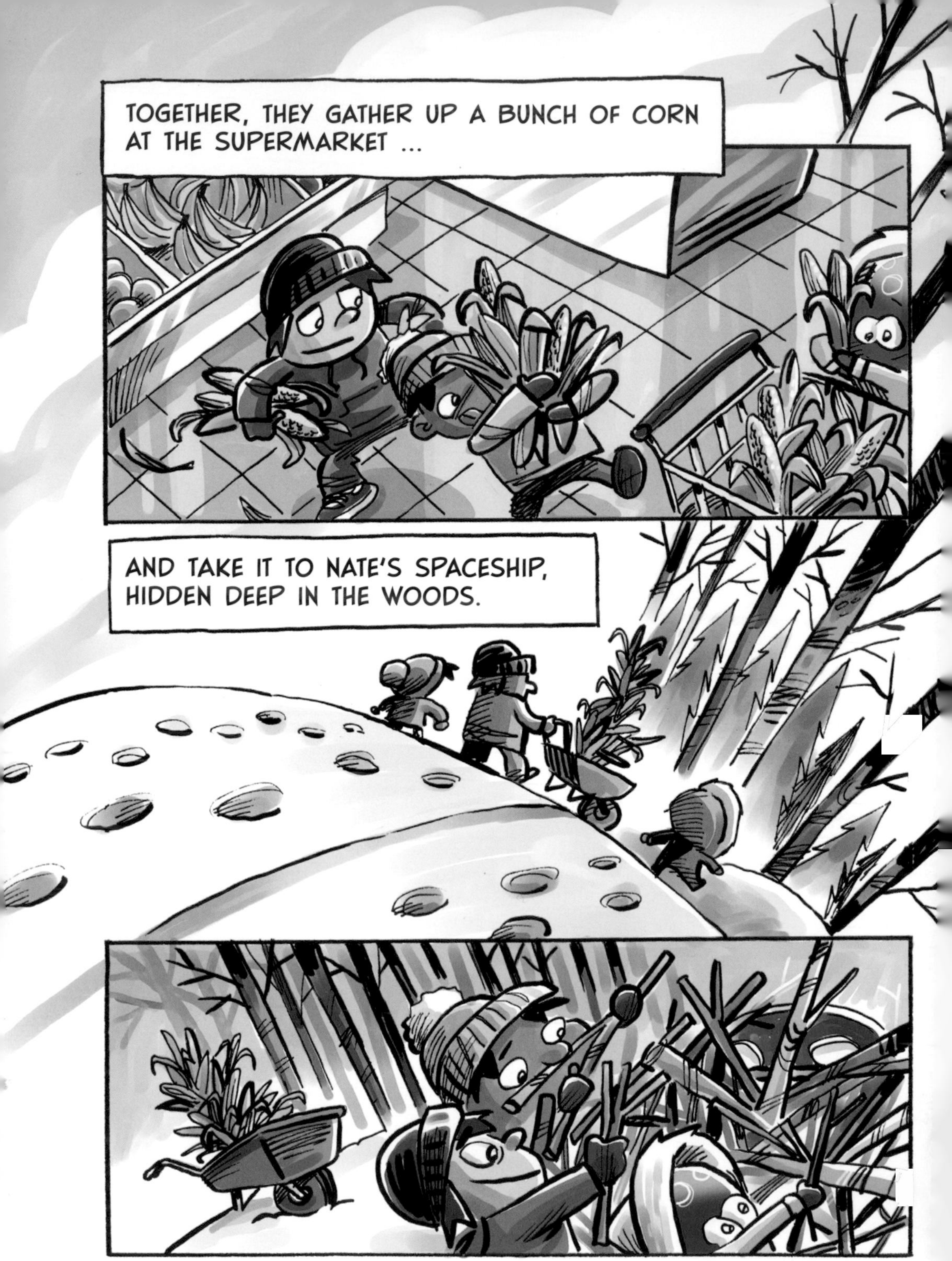
TOGETHER, THEY GATHER UP A BUNCH OF CORN AT THE SUPERMARKET ...
AND TAKE IT TO NATE'S SPACESHIP, HIDDEN DEEP IN THE WOODS.

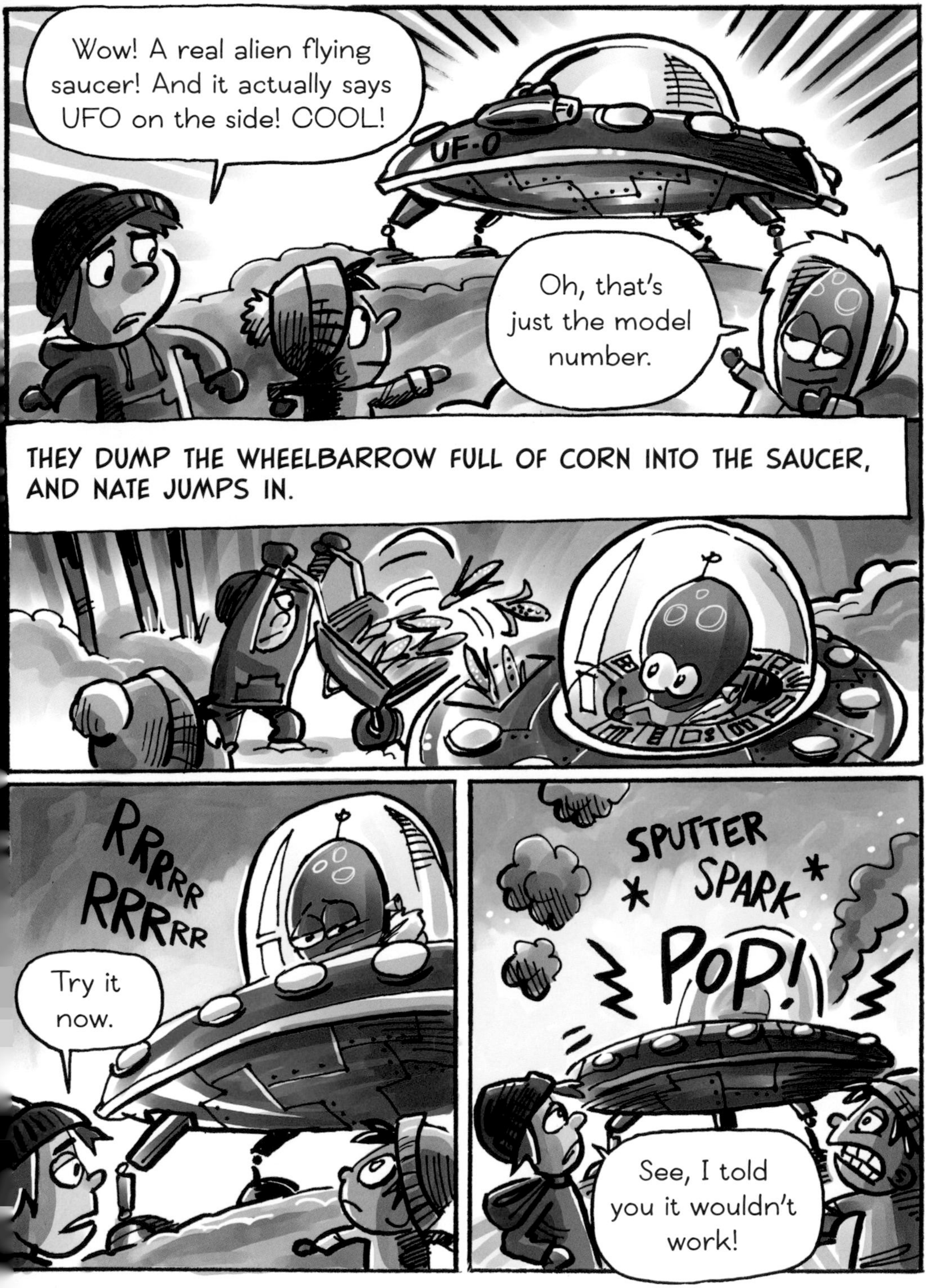
Wow! A real alien flying saucer! And it actually says UFO on the side! COOL!
UF-O
Oh, that's just the model number.
THEY DUMP THE WHEELBARROW FULL OF CORN INTO THE SAUCER, AND NATE JUMPS IN.
RRRRRR RRRRRR
Try it now.
SPUTTER SPARK
POP!
See, I told you it wouldn't work!

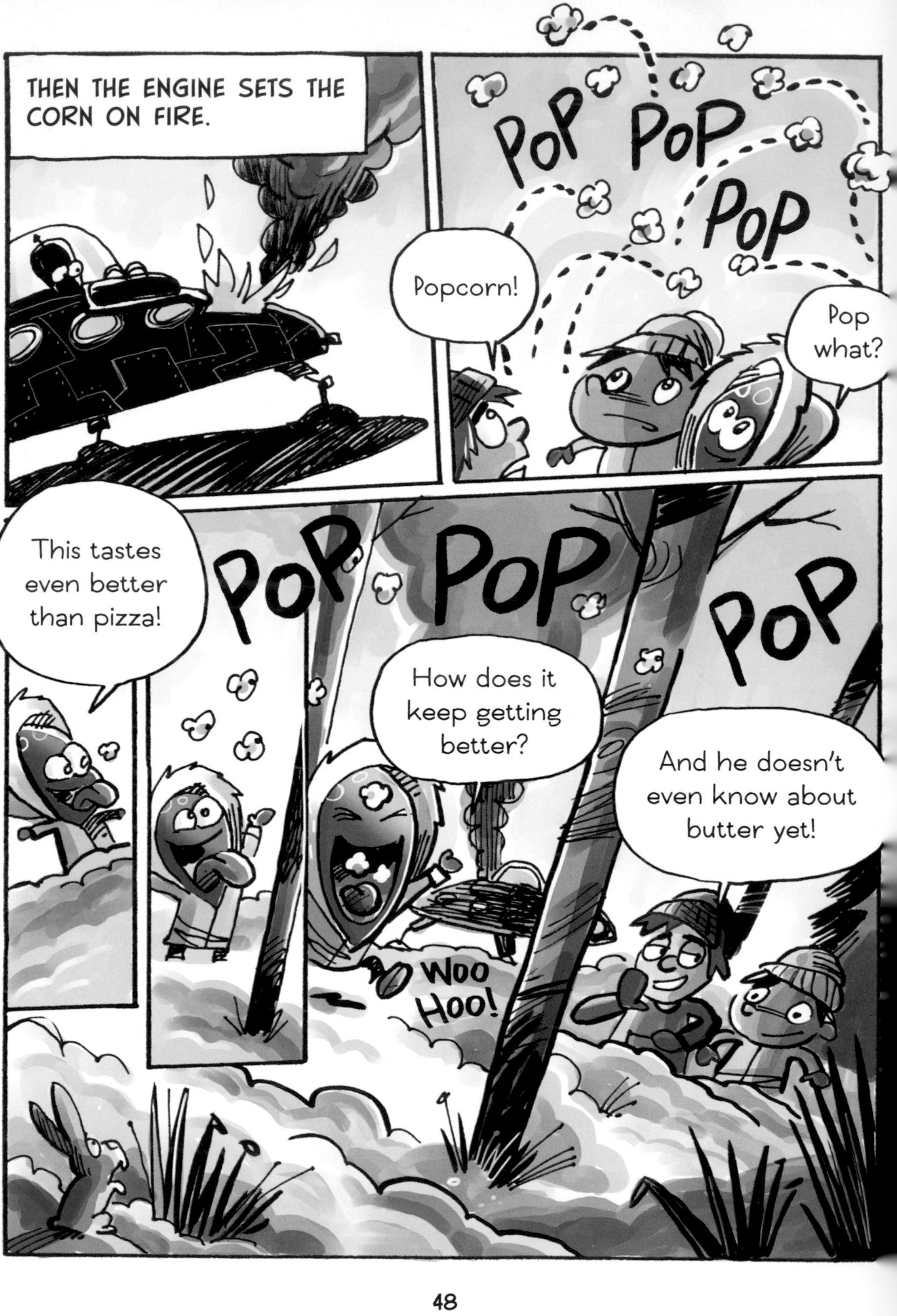
THEN THE ENGINE SETS THE CORN ON FIRE.
POP POP POP
Popcorn!
Pop what?
This tastes even better than pizza!
POP POP POP
How does it keep getting better?
And he doesn't even know about butter yet!
WOO HOO!

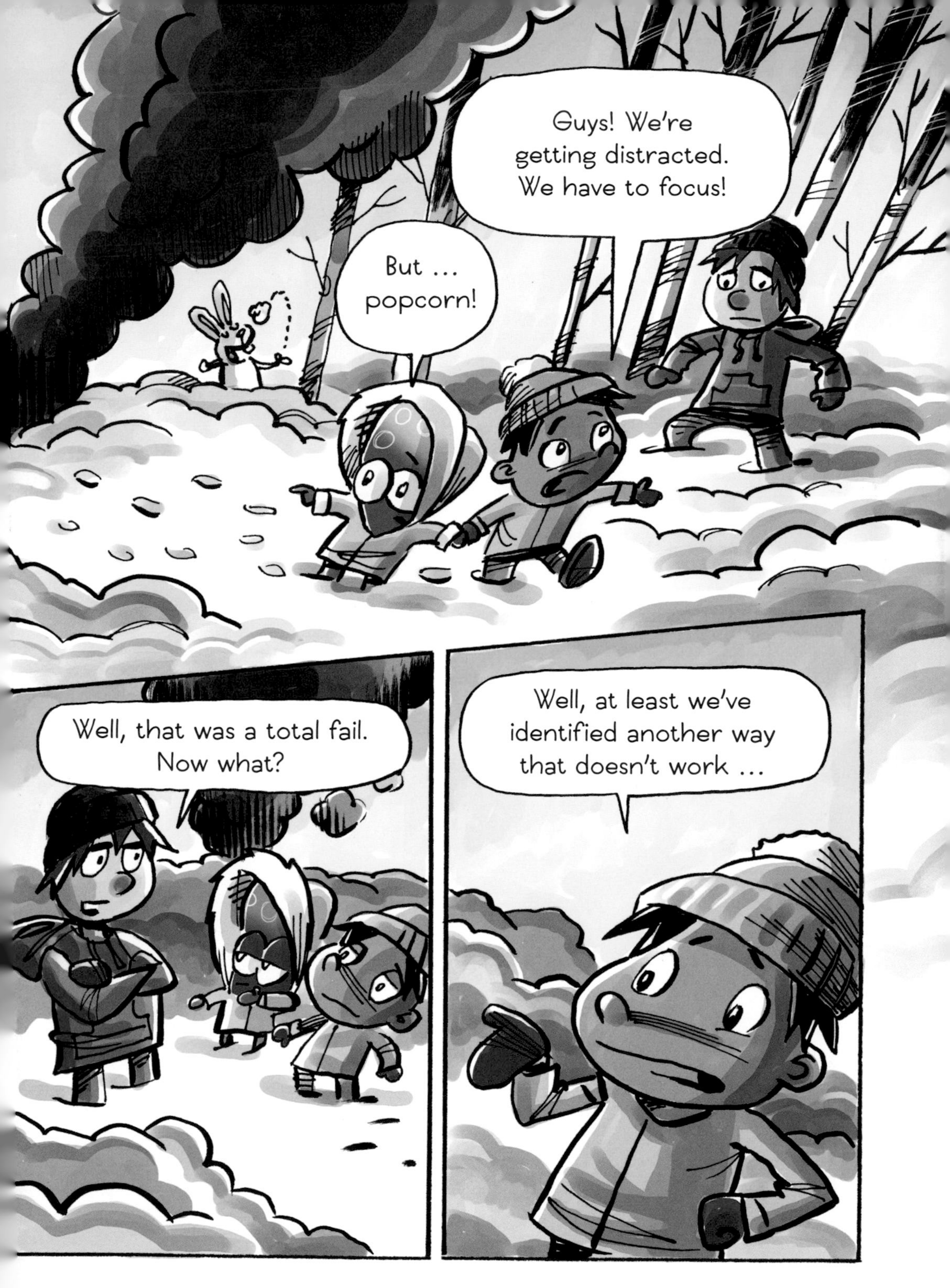

Guys! We're getting distracted. We have to focus!
But ... popcorn!
Well, that was a total fail. Now what?
Well, at least we've identified another way that doesn't work ...

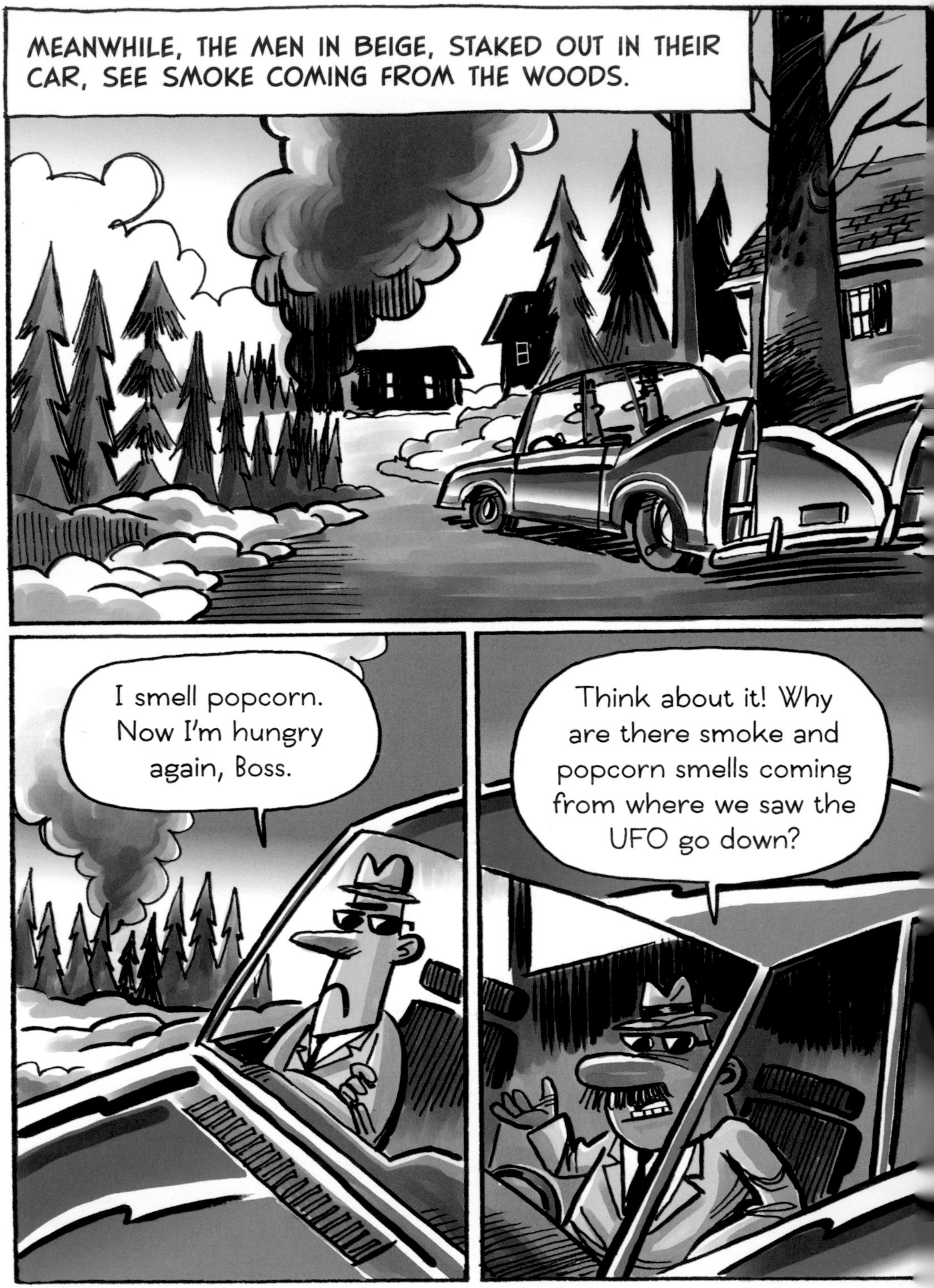
MEANWHILE, THE MEN IN BEIGE, STAKED OUT IN THEIR CAR, SEE SMOKE COMING FROM THE WOODS.
I smell popcorn. Now I'm hungry again, Boss.
Think about it! Why are there smoke and popcorn smells coming from where we saw the UFO go down?

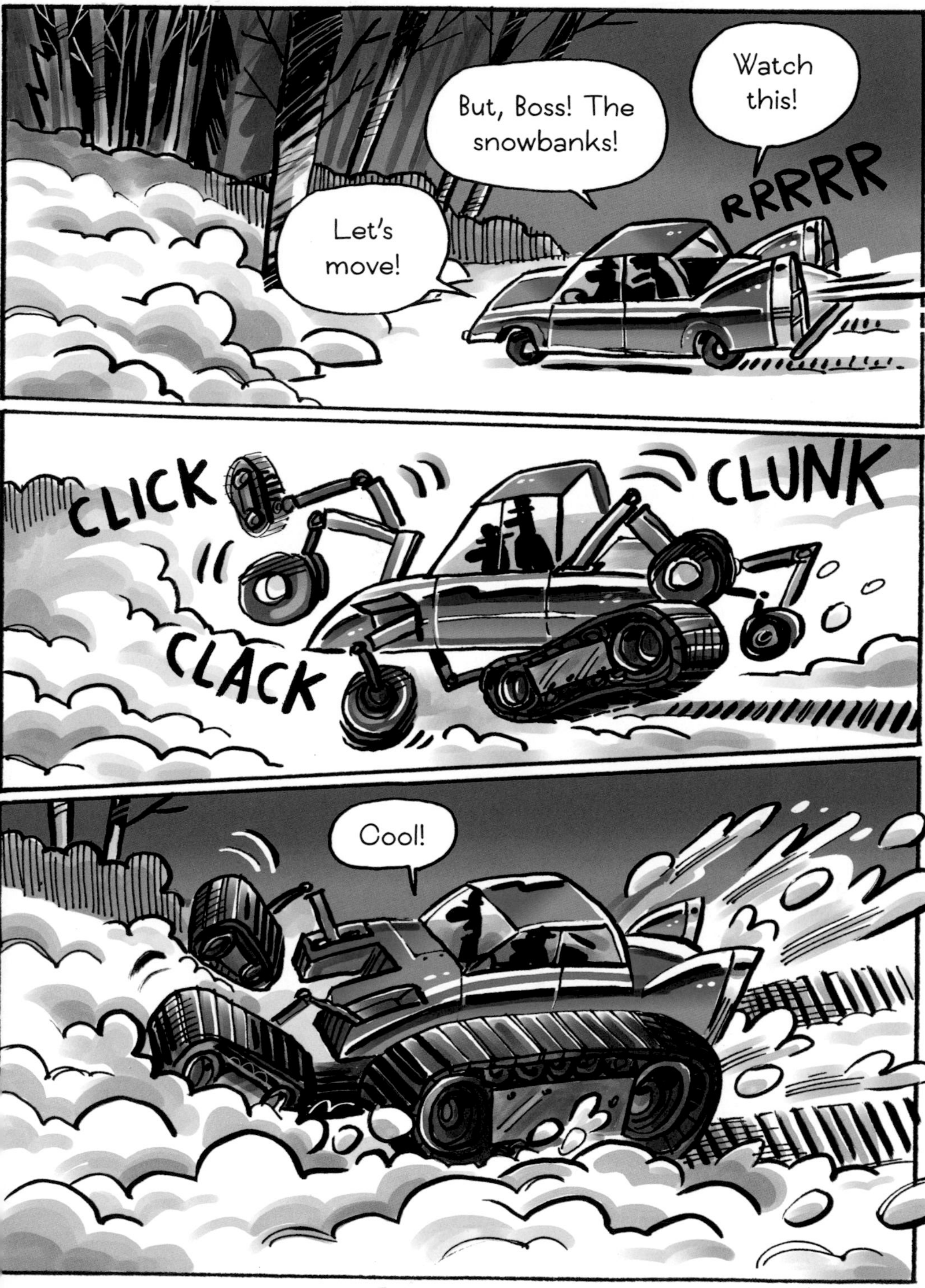
Let's move!
But, Boss! The snowbanks!
Watch this!
RRRRR
CLICK
CLUNK
CLACK
Cool!

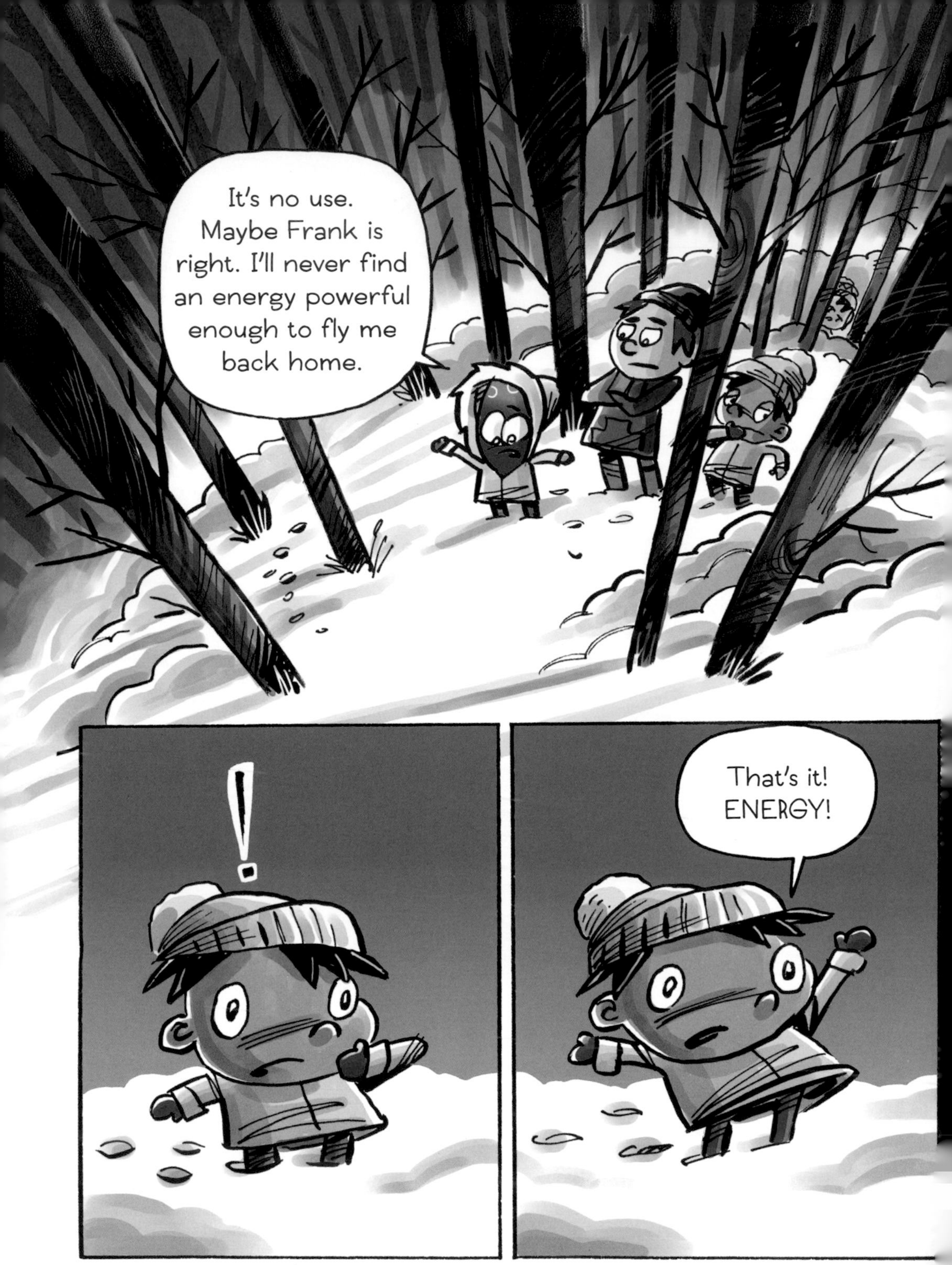
It's no use. Maybe Frank is right. I'll never find an energy powerful enough to fly me back home.
!
That's it! ENERGY!

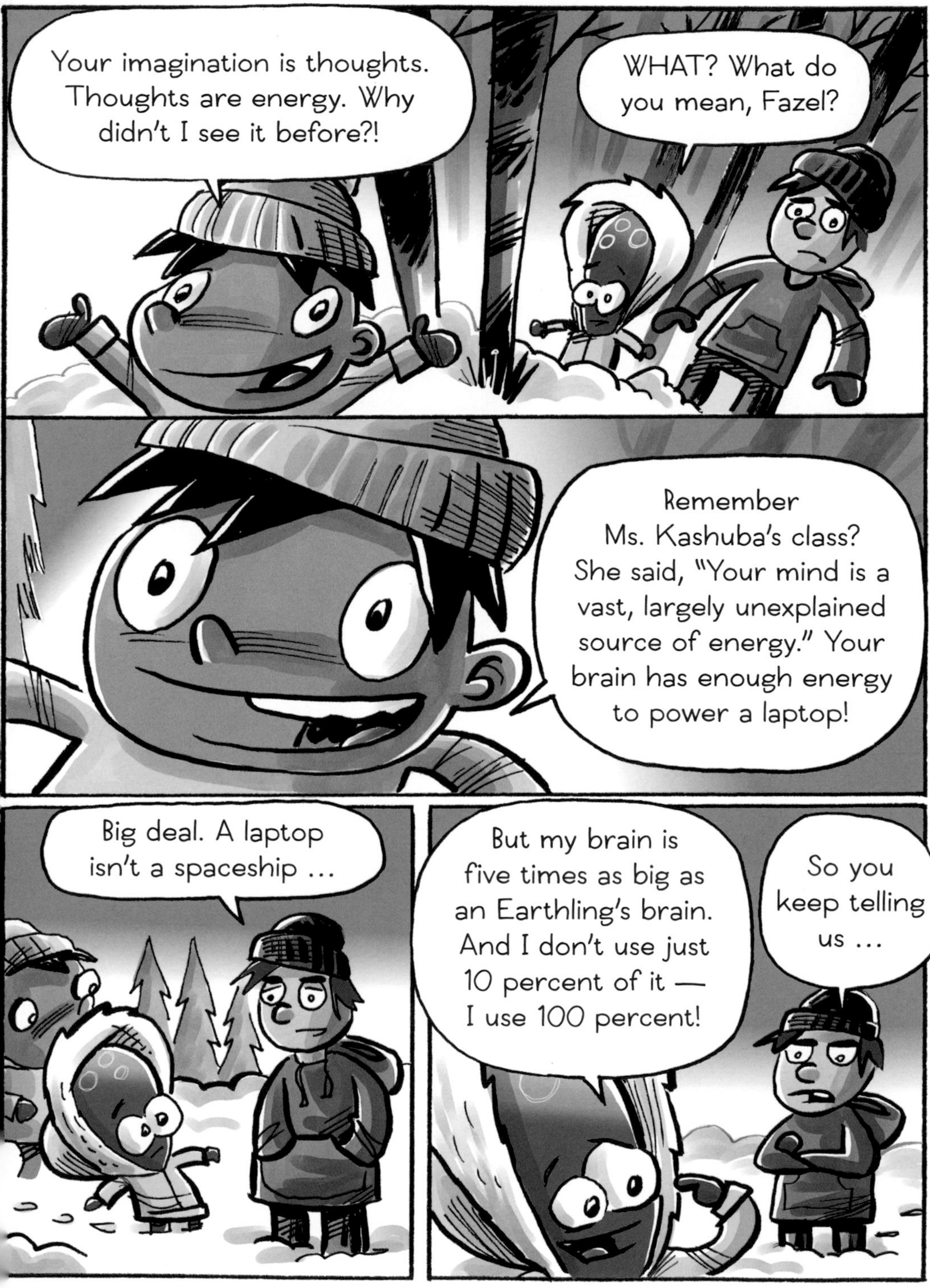
Your imagination is thoughts. Thoughts are energy. Why didn't I see it before?!
WHAT? What do you mean, Fazel?
Remember Ms. Kashuba's class? She said, "Your mind is a vast, largely unexplained source of energy." Your brain has enough energy to power a laptop!
Big deal. A laptop isn't a spaceship ...
But my brain is five times as big as an Earthling's brain. And I don't use just 10 percent of it — I use 100 percent!
So you keep telling us ...

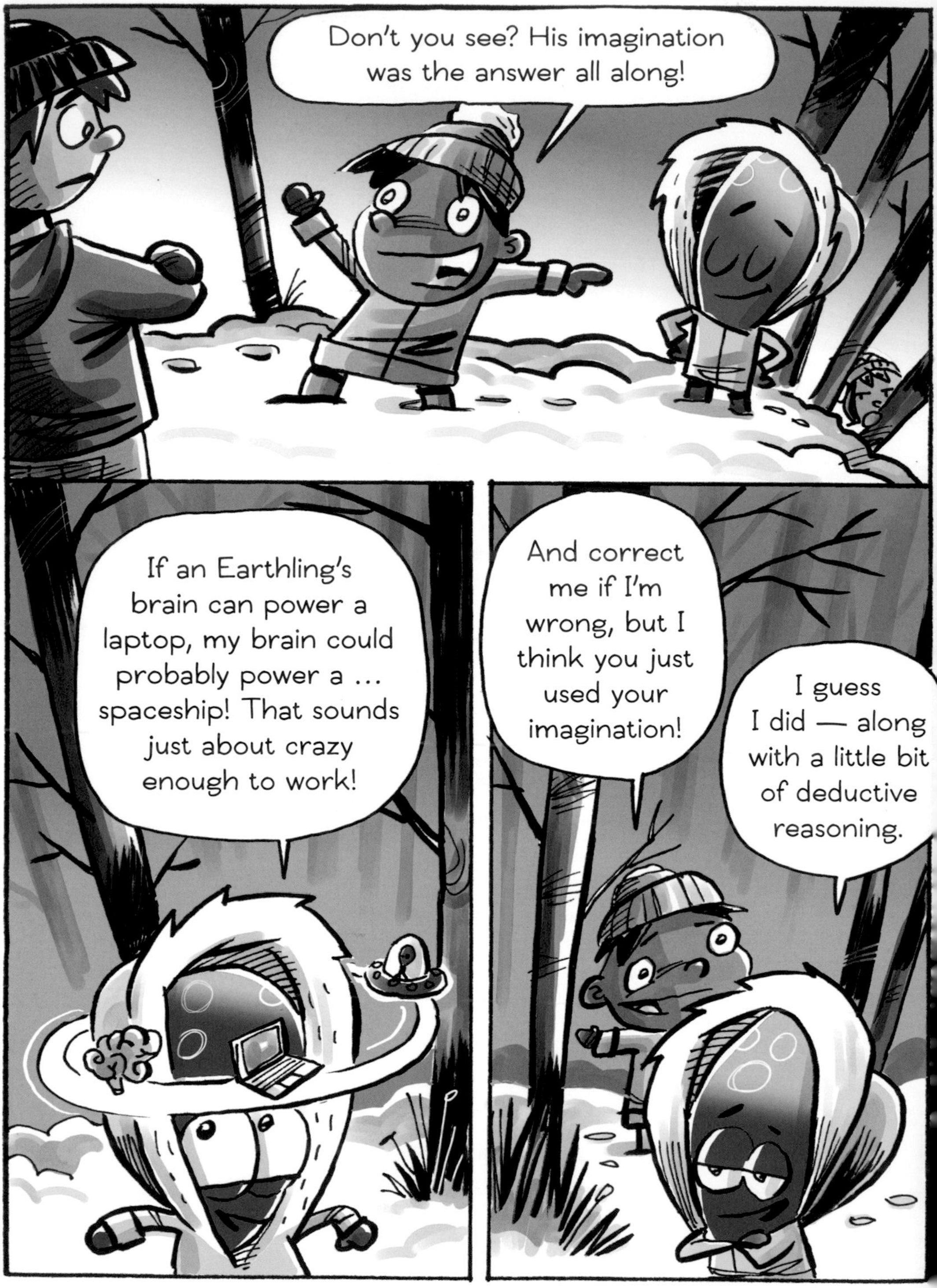
Don't you see? His imagination was the answer all along!
If an Earthling's brain can power a laptop, my brain could probably power a ... spaceship! That sounds just about crazy enough to work!
And correct me if I'm wrong, but I think you just used your imagination!
I guess I did — along with a little bit of deductive reasoning.

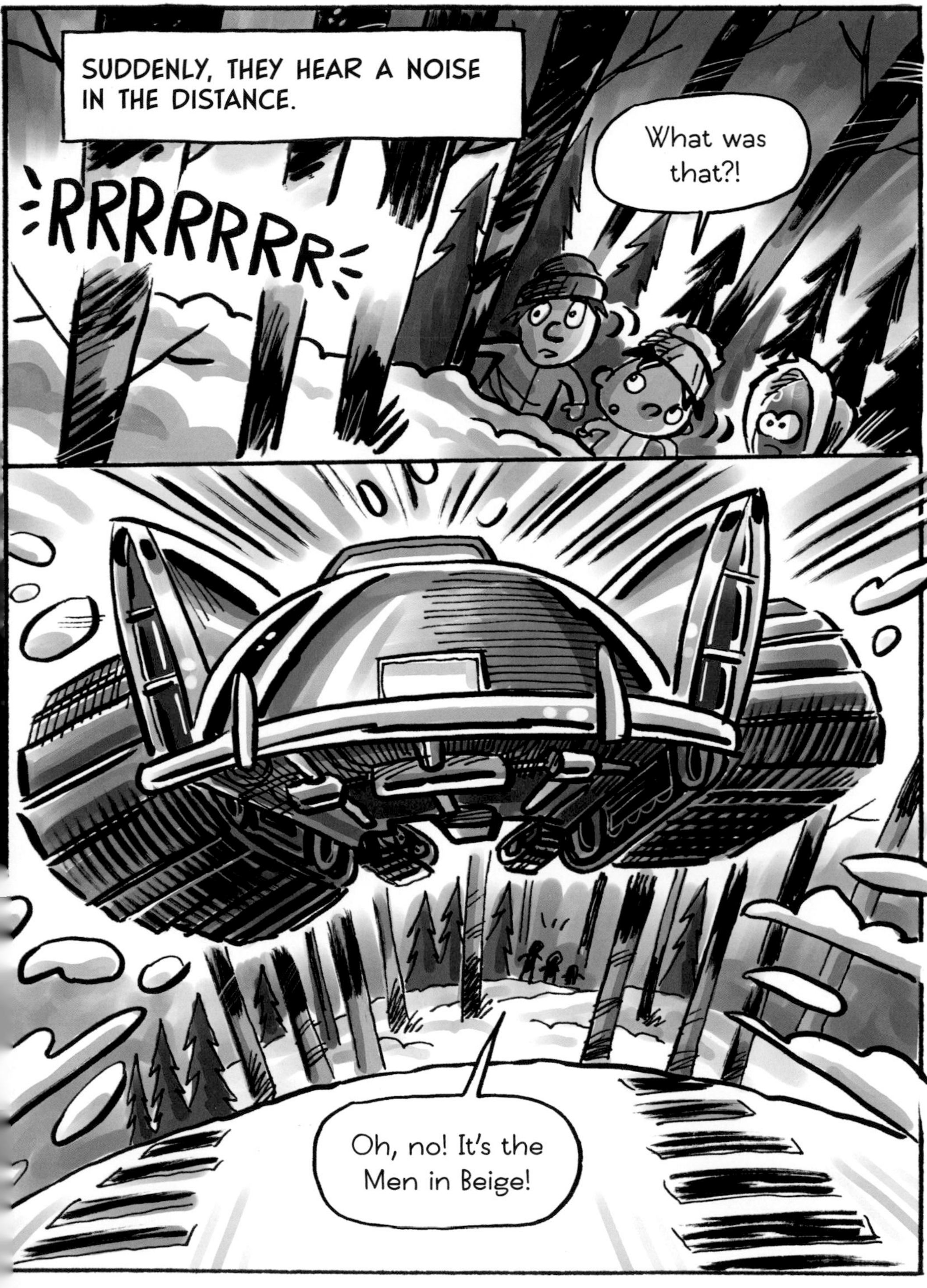
SUDDENLY, THEY HEAR A NOISE IN THE DISTANCE.
RRRRRRRR
What was that?!
Oh, no! It's the Men in Beige!

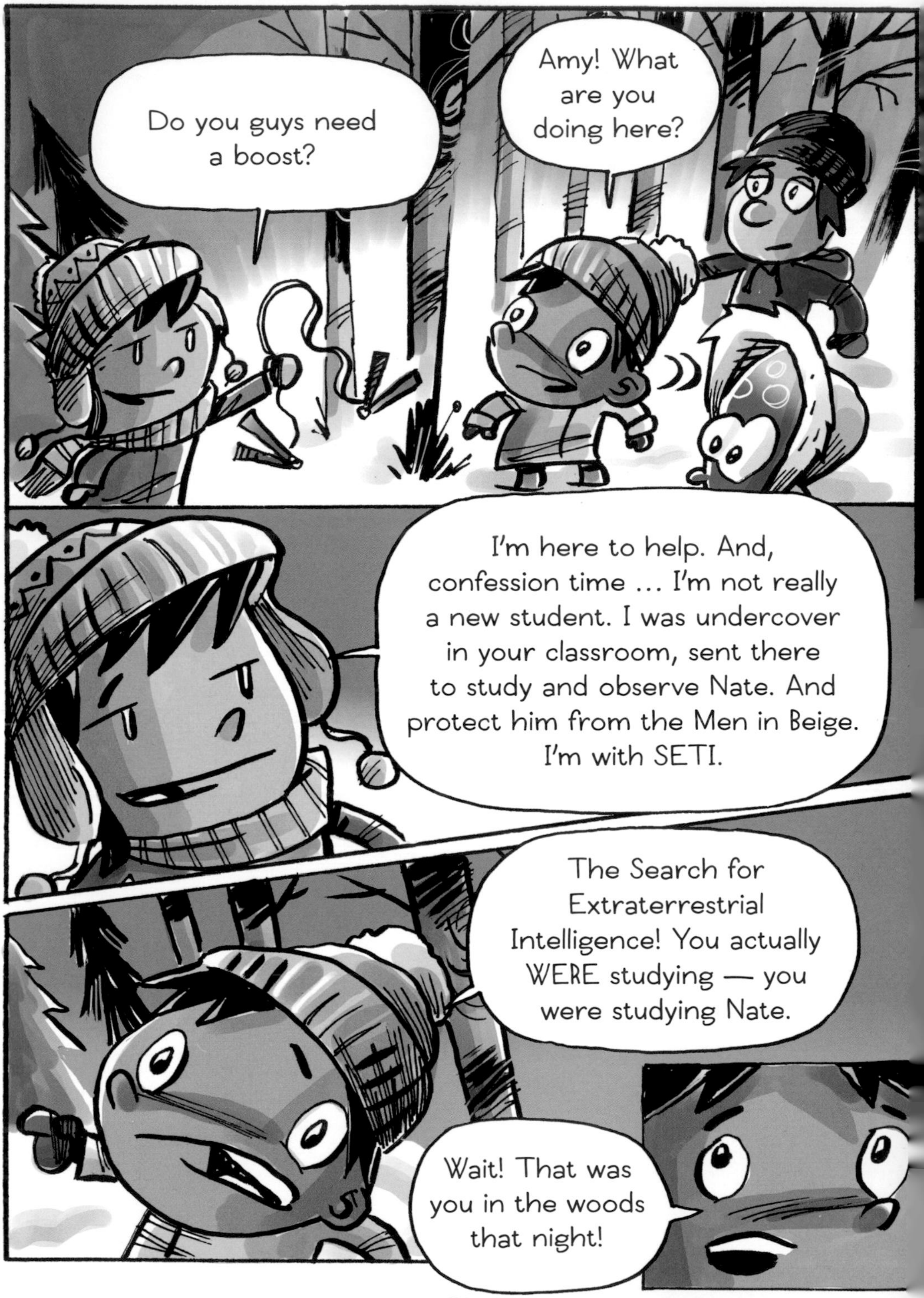
Do you guys need a boost?
Amy! What are you doing here?
I'm here to help. And, confession time ... I'm not really a new student. I was undercover in your classroom, sent there to study and observe Nate. And protect him from the Men in Beige. I'm with SETI.
The Search for Extraterrestrial Intelligence! You actually WERE studying — you were studying Nate.
Wait! That was you in the woods that night!

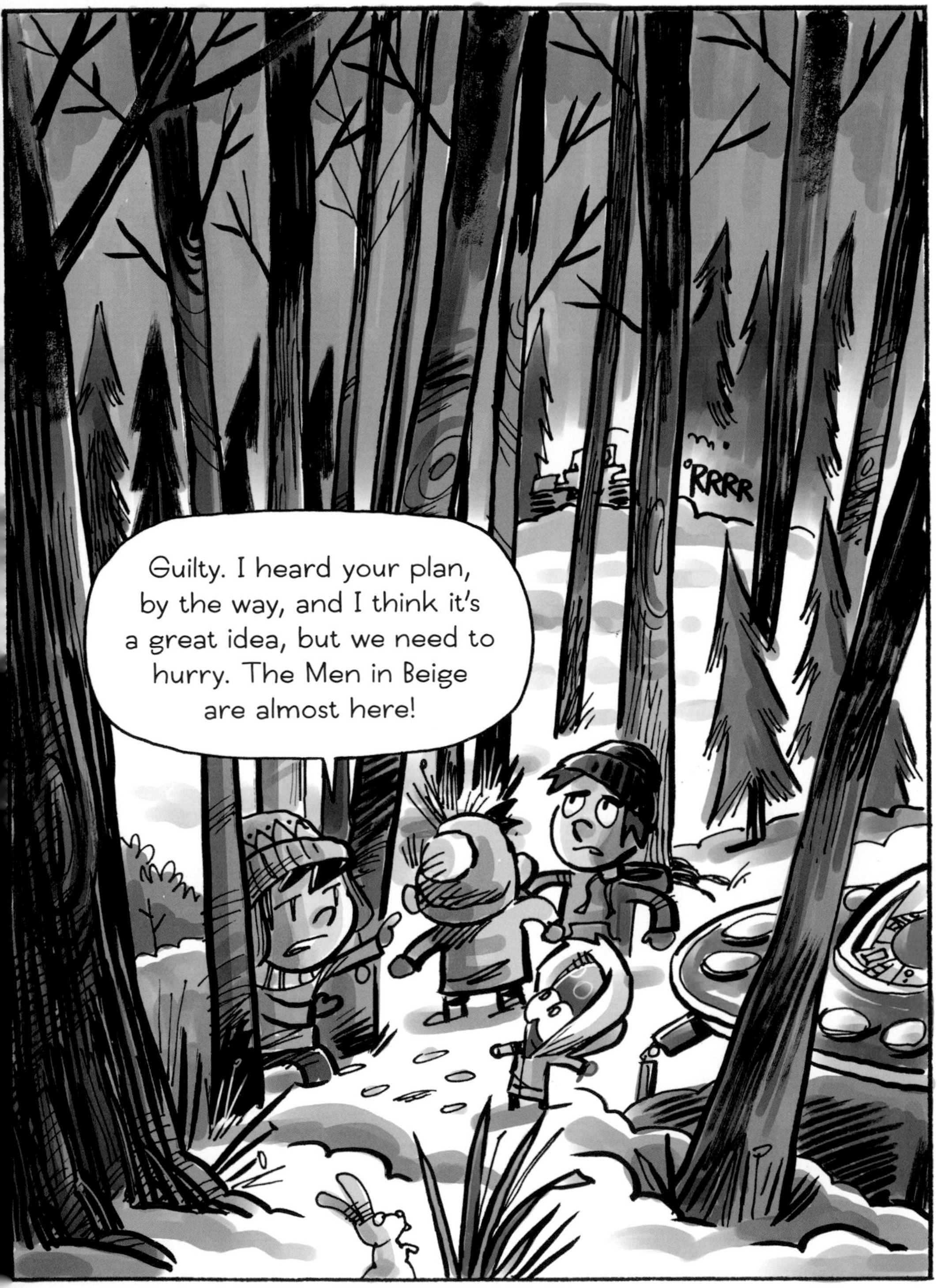

RRRR
Guilty. I heard your plan, by the way, and I think it's a great idea, but we need to hurry. The Men in Beige are almost here!

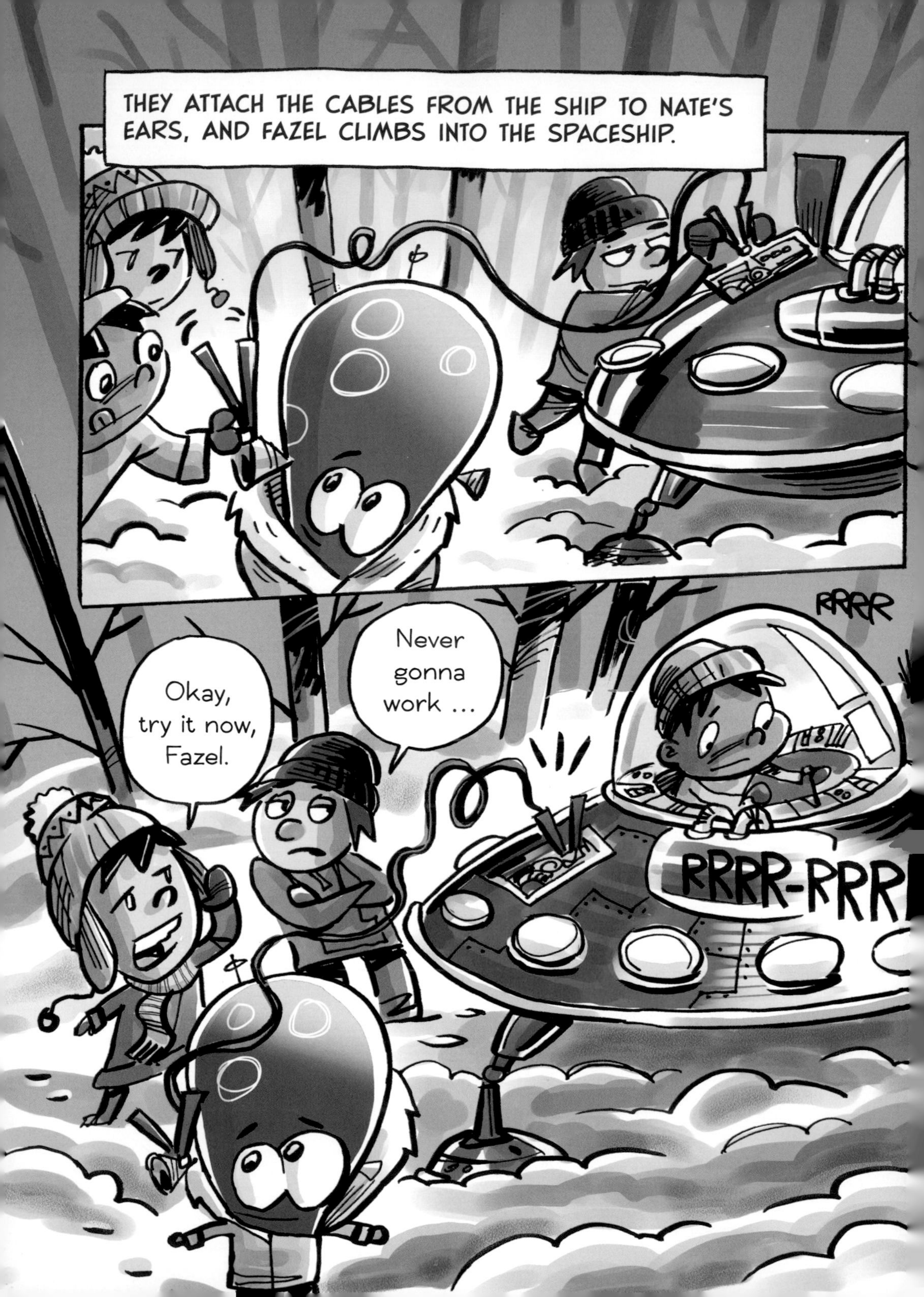
THEY ATTACH THE CABLES FROM THE SHIP TO NATE'S EARS, AND FAZEL CLIMBS INTO THE SPACESHIP.
RRRR
Okay, try it now, Fazel.
Never gonna work ...
RRRR-RRR

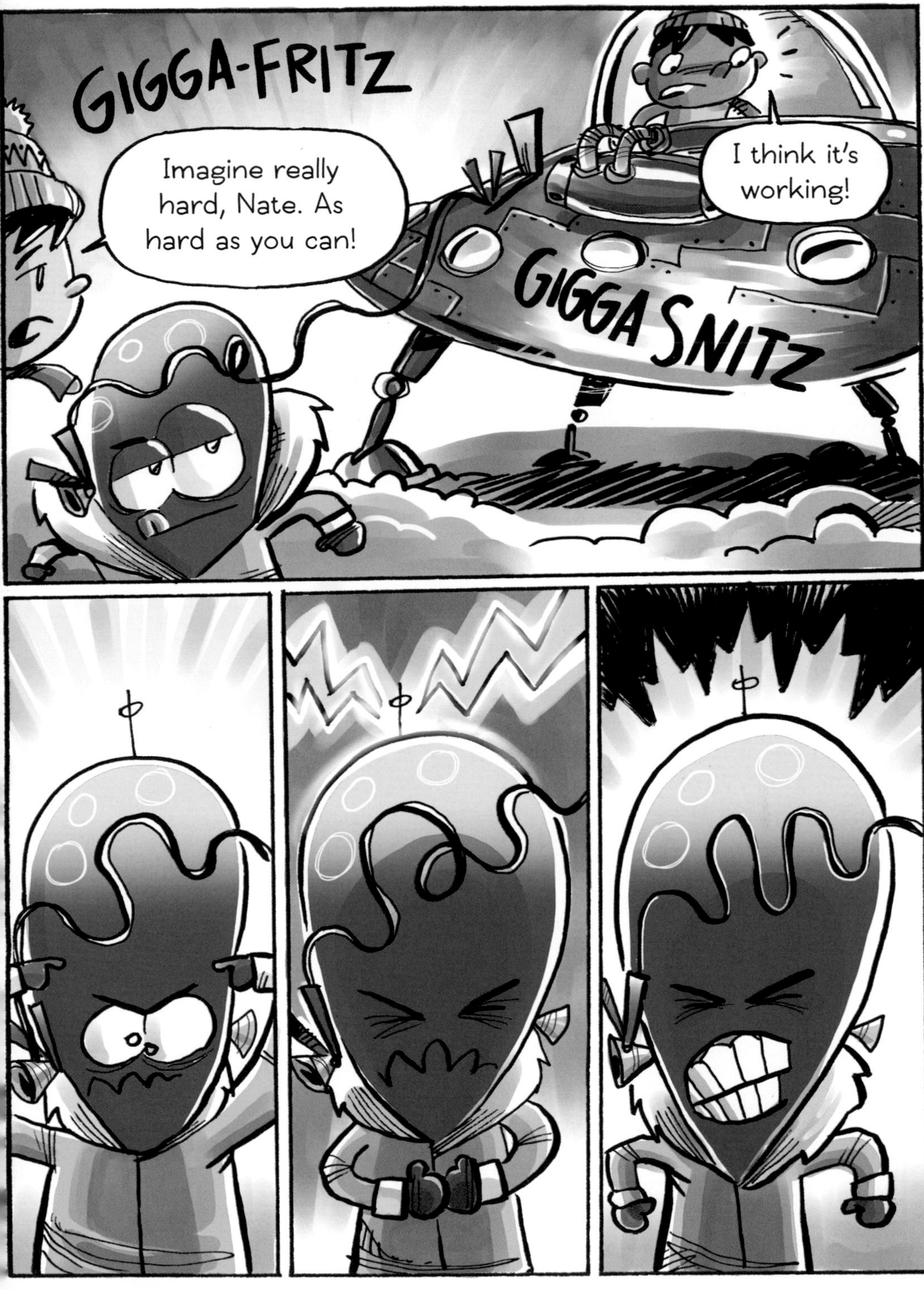
GIGGA-FRITZ
Imagine really hard, Nate. As hard as you can!
I think it's working!
GIGGA SNITZ

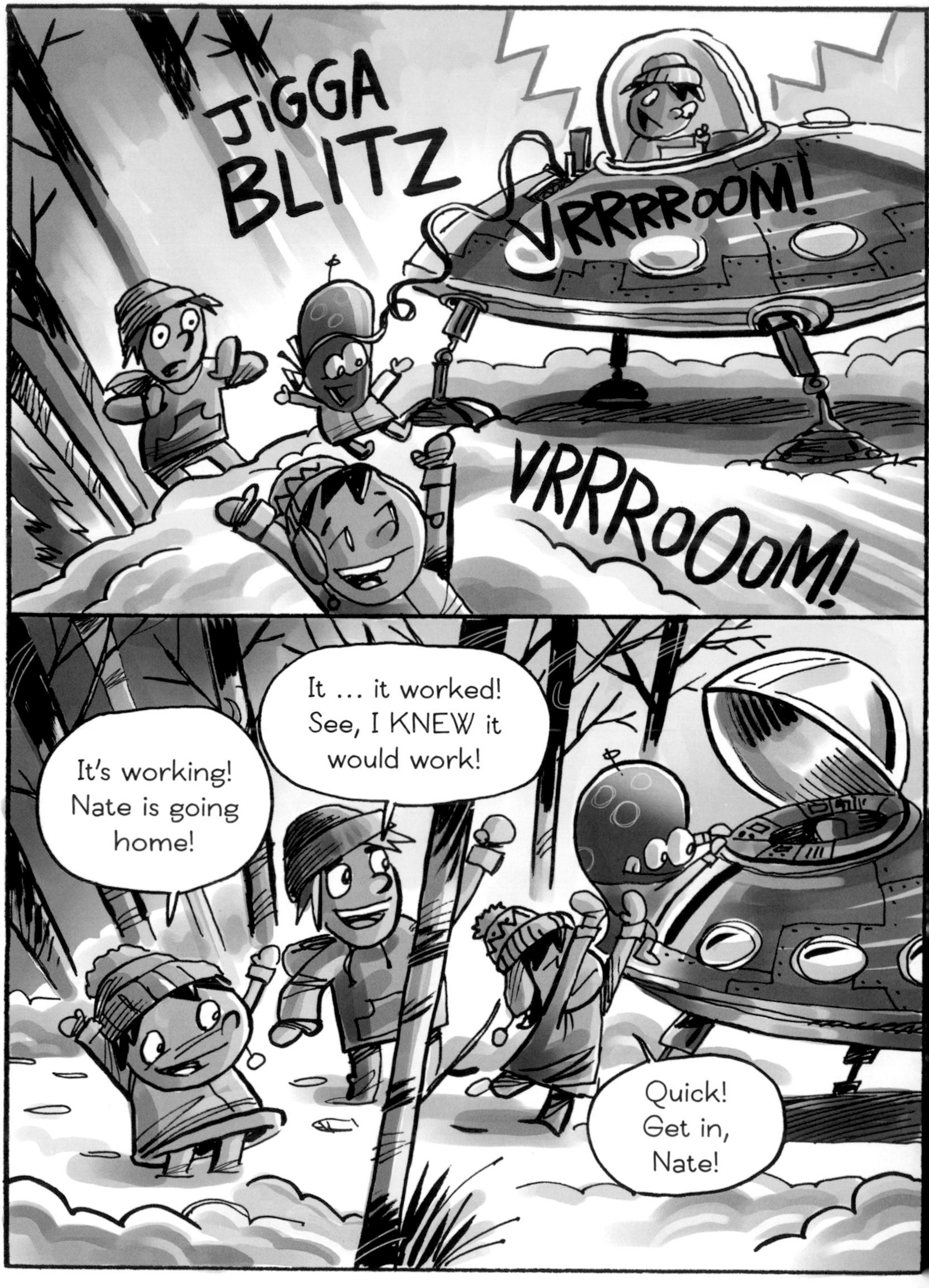
JIGGA
BLITZ
VRRRROOM!
VRRROOOOM!
It's working! Nate is going home!
It ... it worked! See, I KNEW it would work!
Quick! Get in, Nate!

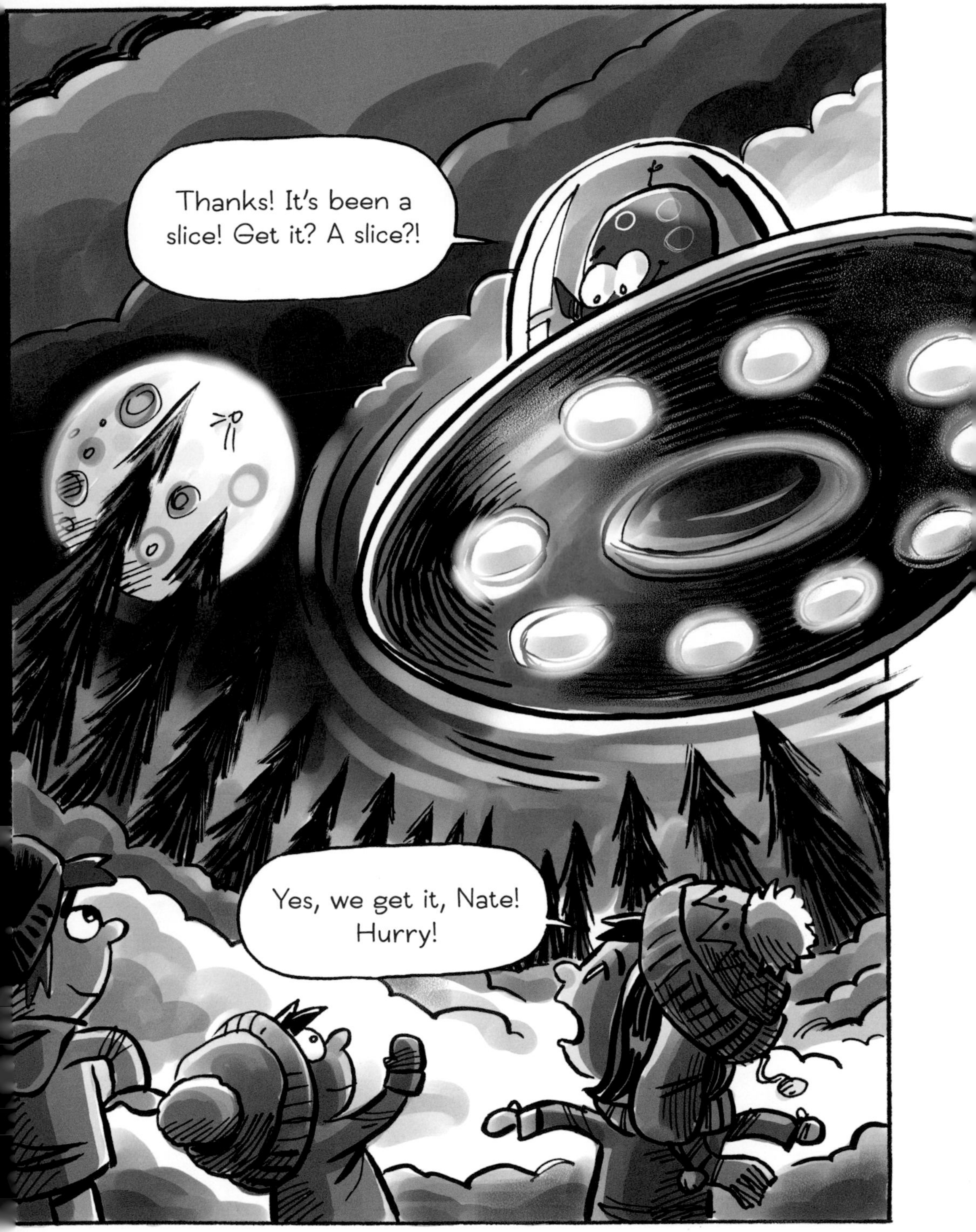
Thanks! It's been a slice! Get it? A slice?!
Yes, we get it, Nate! Hurry!

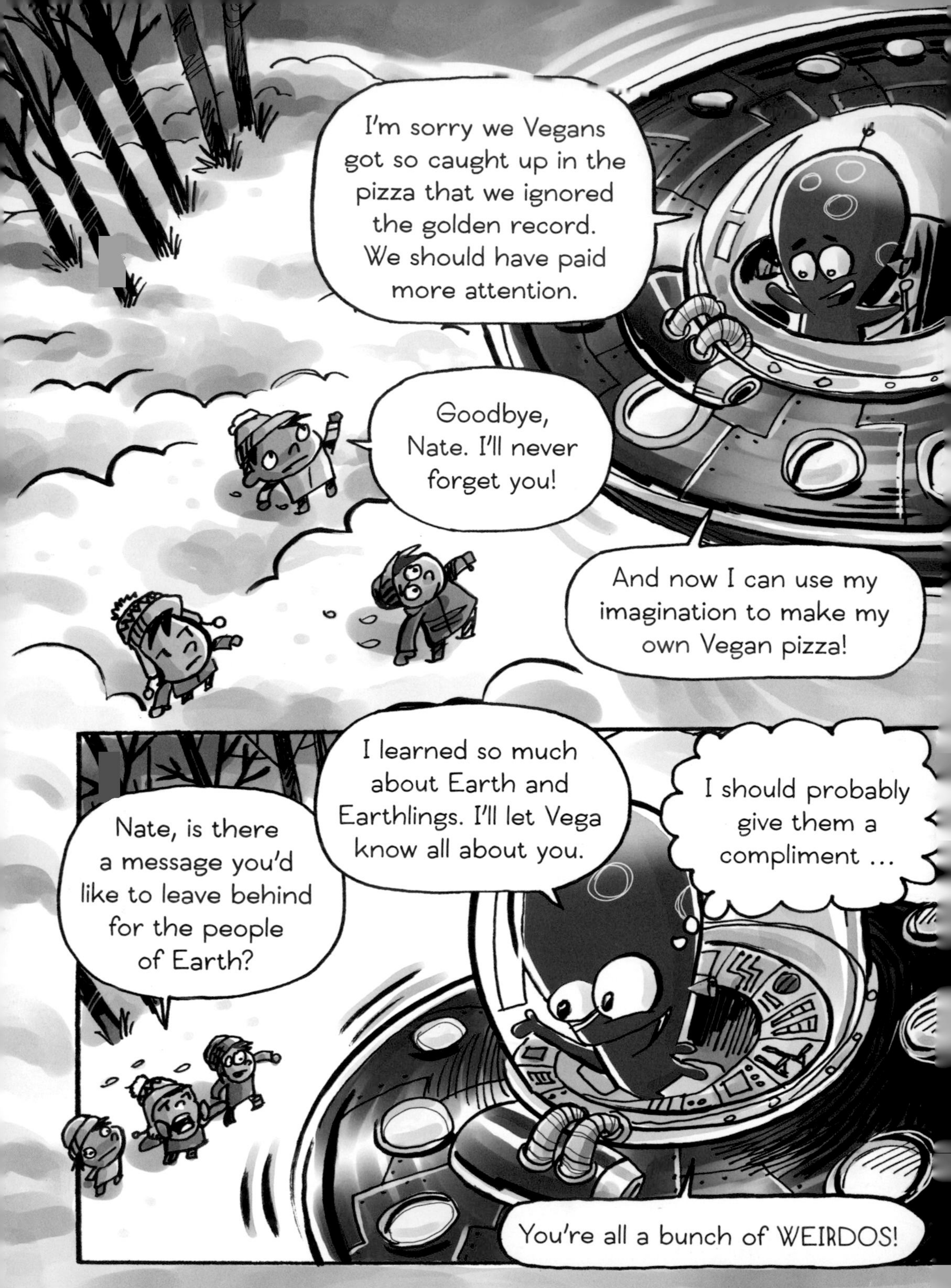
I'm sorry we Vegans got so caught up in the pizza that we ignored the golden record. We should have paid more attention.
Goodbye, Nate. I'll never forget you!
And now I can use my imagination to make my own Vegan pizza!
I learned so much about Earth and Earthlings. I'll let Vega know all about you.
Nate, is there a message you'd like to leave behind for the people of Earth?
I should probably give them a compliment ...
You're all a bunch of WEIRDOS!

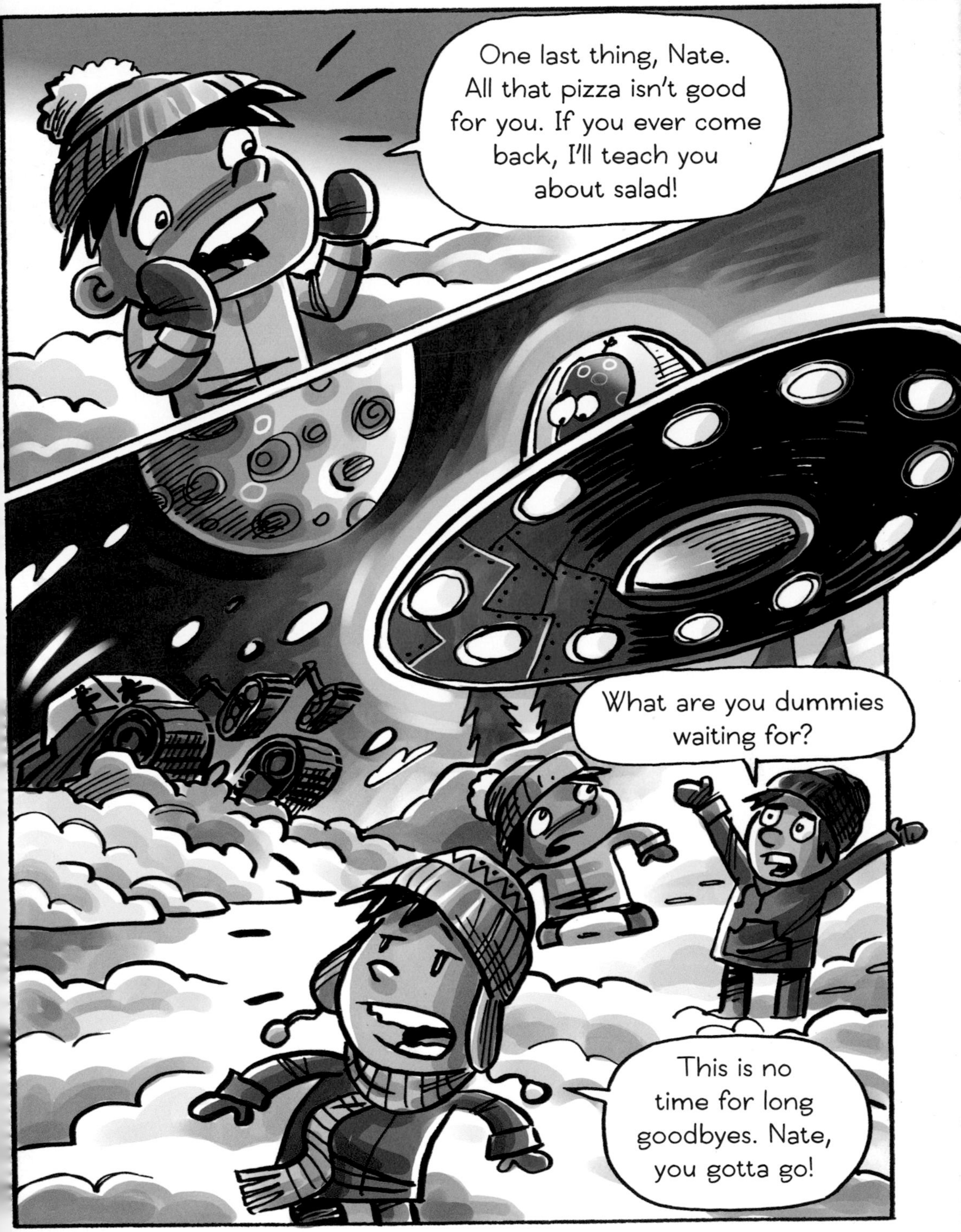
One last thing, Nate. All that pizza isn't good for you. If you ever come back, I'll teach you about salad!
What are you dummies waiting for?
This is no time for long goodbyes. Nate, you gotta go!

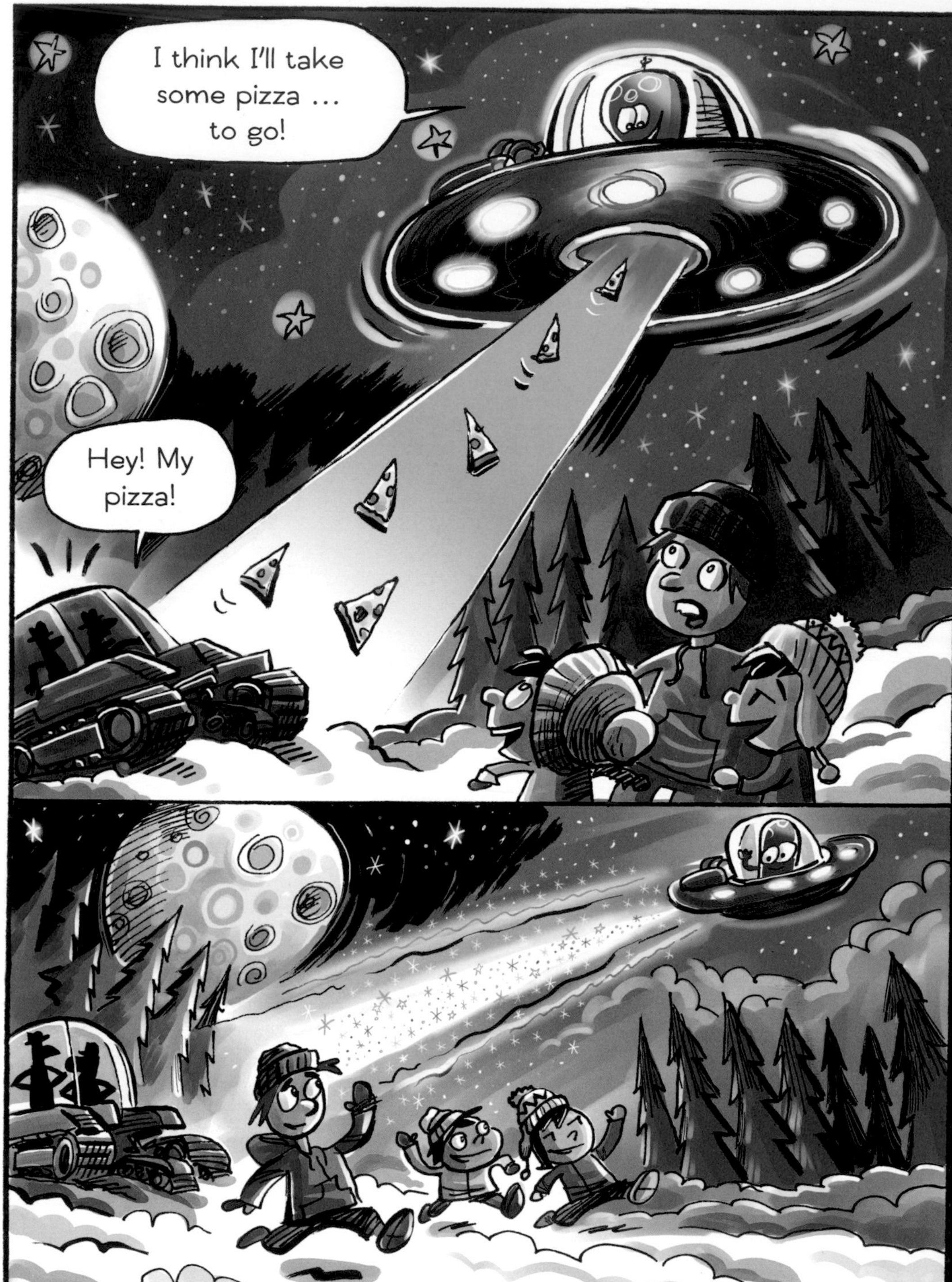
I think I'll take some pizza ... to go!
Hey! My pizza!